LUIGI FERRO
BOARDING MURDER

Luigi Ferro
Boarding Murder
Story by Matt Borne
Copyright © 2024
Cover by Mats Ingelborn
Photos by A.Karnaushenko, Kiuikson & Wirestock
ISBN print: 978-91-89822-53-5
ISBN e-book: 978-91-89822-54-2
Published by Yabot AB, Sweden, 2024

1

The sun had started to descend over the mountains, casting long shadows over the microstate of San Marino. I sat in my cramped office, pouring over the last details of a minor case involving a stolen gold pocket watch. The whole fiasco turned out to be nothing more than a jealous lover's attempt at revenge – a tale as old as time itself.

"Signor Ferro," a timid voice called through the door, "I... I have your payment."

The door creaked open, revealing a young man with a red face and trembling hands. He held out an envelope stuffed with cash, the weight of the bills heavy with both relief and regret.

"Thank you, ragazzo," I said, taking the money with a nod. "Let this be a lesson for the future. Trust is a delicate thing – don't let jealousy blind you to what truly matters."

The young man nodded, his eyes glistening with unshed tears, and then slipped away into the fading light.

As the door clicked shut behind him, I savored the final moments of victory before it all dissolved back into the chaos of life. Cases like these were the bread and butter of my profession, but they left me hungry for something deeper, something that would challenge my intellect and awaken the dormant desires that lay hidden beneath my hard-boiled exterior.

That evening, I found myself at my favorite taverna, seeking solace in the familiar smells of garlic and fresh tomatoes. The place was a sanctuary for me, a respite from the chaos and deceit that often swirled around my profession.

Slipping into a shadowy table by the far wall, I waved to Fabio, the taverna's owner, and soon found a glass of rich, velvety red wine before me. The taste of dark cherries and spice lingered on my tongue like a lover's whisper, tempting and intoxicating.

I leaned back against the worn wooden chair and surveyed the room with a practiced eye. Twilight pooled in the corners and crept lazily across the rough wooden floor as couples huddled together at candlelit tables, their laughter spilling out like coins from a gambler's purse. For once, I found myself alone at the taverna, my usual companion – Caterina, the fiery beauty from SMTV – occupied with her work. The absence of her presence was a dull ache that settled in my chest, but I pushed it aside. Solitude could be my mistress tonight.

Through the window, I watched as pretty Italian women strolled by, their skirts swirling around their legs like dark secrets. Desire stirred within me, a familiar and dangerous hunger, but I remained rooted to my spot, letting temptation wash over me like waves upon the shore. There was something about the serene beauty of San Marino that made even the darkness seem alluring, seductive in its own way.

"Life is full of mysteries, isn't it, Signor Ferro?" Fabio asked, his voice barely audible above the murmur of the patrons.

"Indeed," I replied, taking another sip of wine. "And it's those mysteries that keep me coming back for more."

As night descended over San Marino, I savored a delicious meal but felt that the calm was merely an illusion, a brief respite before the storm. For in this world of shadows and secrets, there was always another case waiting just around the corner.

I suddenly noticed that the clatter of the restaurant faded into a hush as my focus was eclipsed by a captivating presence a few tables away. She was an embodiment of allure, her beauty resonating in the dimly lit room like a soft, unmistakable melody. I found myself entranced, my seasoned detective's gaze softened by her charm.

Her lips, a perfect blend of boldness and grace, had curved gently, whispering secrets of a vivacious spirit. Every time she smiled, the room seemed to brighten, casting a spell that was hard to ignore. I was drawn in, wondering what stories those lips could tell, what mysteries they might conceal.

The cascade of her dark hair had framed her face like a portrait of elegance, each strand a testament to a natural, effortless allure. It had fallen over her shoulders, a dark river shimmering under the subtle lights, inviting yet unattainable.

Her attire spoke of sophistication – a blend of style and comfort. It had accentuated her form, revealing a confidence that was as striking as her physical beauty. And then, those legs – shapely, poised, the very definition of grace. They had carried her with an ease that spoke of a quiet strength, a harmony of movement that was captivating.

At that moment, lost in her beauty, the mysteries I usually chased had seemed trivial. She was an enigma, a story untold, a mystery not to be solved but admired from the respectful distance of my table.

An abrupt and annoying signal from a cell phone snapped me from the daydream. It was my own phone, and I glared at it as I pulled it from my pocket. An unknown number. It wasn't often that my solitary musings were interrupted; who dared breach my sanctuary?

"Pronto," I grunted into the device, sounding more irritated than I was.

"Signor Luigi Ferro?" an unfamiliar female voice queried.

"Yes. Who is this?" I asked, the timbre of my voice low and measured.

"Buona sera, Signor Ferro," continued the tremulous voice on the other end of the line. "I am Madame Merola, calling from the Umbri International School in Ravenna."

"Ravenna?" I echoed, arching an eyebrow, curiosity beginning to stir beneath my calm exterior.

"I am the headmistress of the boarding school. Signor Ferro, there has been a...a terrible incident. A student, a young girl from Switzerland, has been murdered during a night out. We need your help," she stammered, her distress palpable through the phone.

"Murder most foul," I mused, the weight of her words settling like a shroud around my shoulders.

Ravenna's history, rich with shades of Byzantine opulence, now marred by a more modern stain.

"Please, Signor Ferro," she begged, desperation tingeing her voice. "I know you have a reputation for unraveling even the most complex of cases. This is a very delicate matter…I implore you to help us find justice for this poor girl."

I paused, swirling the wine in my glass, the liquid's slow dance a mirror for my thoughts. The temptation of the case was undeniable – another mystery beckoning me into its shadowy embrace. But along with it came the inherent dangers; those who sought to silence the truth were often ruthless in their pursuit.

"Her name was Alicia Hodler, Swiss by birth, with a family as wealthy as the Medici themselves," she continued, her words painting a portrait of privilege and power. "She was an exceptional student, admired by both her peers and teachers alike, and her death has cast a pall over the entire school."

"Very well, Madame Merola," I finally acquiesced, sensing an irresistible challenge and compelled by the urgency in her voice. "I will come to Ravenna and lend my expertise to your cause."

"Thank you, Signor Ferro," she breathed, relief sighing through the line. "You don't know how much this means to us."

"Sure," I replied cryptically, hanging up, but I did not put the phone back in my pocket. The evening's tranquility shattered, replaced by the seductive whisper of the unknown, daring me to step once more into the abyss.

Before setting out, I knew it was prudent to gather whatever intel I could on the Umbri International School and the ill-fated Alicia Hodler. I turned my attention to the cell phone again, its screen casting a cold glow upon my face as my fingers danced across the screen, delving into the digital realm that held a wealth of knowledge at my fingertips.

"Umbri International School," I murmured, sifting through the search results. The institution boasted an impressive reputation, housed within an 18th-century palazzo in central Ravenna. A veritable fortress of academia, it catered to the children of the elite – a fertile breeding ground for the ambitions and desires that defined their world.

"Ah, Alicia Hodler," I said, my voice steeped in melancholy as I gazed upon her image. She was young and beautiful, with blonde hair cascading like golden silk down her back and eyes that seemed to hold the innocence of youth within their azure depths. A tragedy, that one so full of potential, should meet such a grisly end.

"Swiss family," I noted, my eyes narrowing as I traced the lines of power and influence that wove their way through Alicia's background. Wealthy, well-connected, and with a proclivity for discretion – the very qualities that would make this case both challenging and irresistible.

Having gathered what information I could, I pocketed the device and took one last sip of my wine. I left behind the sanctuary of the taverna, the night air wrapping itself around me like the delicate nylon of

Caterina's stockings – a tactile memory that threatened to unravel me. As I embarked upon this treacherous journey, the intoxicating allure of secrets and shadows seduced me once more, a siren song that promised darkness, desire, and a dance with danger.

*

"Be careful, Luigi," Caterina whispered to me in the morning, her lush mouth grazing my earlobe as she fastened the cufflinks that bore my initials. Her concern, though touching, was tinged with a hint of bitterness – the taste of jealousy soured by the knowledge that she could never fully possess me. For I belonged not to her, nor to any other woman, but to the shadows that called me forth from the depths of my soul.

"Always, darling," I replied, brushing my lips against her temple and inhaling the intoxicating scent of her perfume. "It is the only way I know how to live."

I assembled my armor for the battle ahead. I reached for a shirt in Egyptian cotton, feeling the tantalizing caress of the fabric against my fingers as I folded it meticulously into my overnight bag. A charcoal suit followed, expertly tailored to accentuate the raw power that lay beneath my unassuming exterior. Above all, one must never underestimate the potency of a well-dressed man.

Discerning eyes would seek out my every weakness, probing for vulnerabilities with the rapacious hunger of a predator. And so, I armed myself accordingly, selecting a collection of tools designed to deceive and beguile even the most astute observer. A lock pick set, disguised as an innocuous pen; a concealed camera, small enough to escape notice, yet powerful enough to pierce the veil of even the most closely guarded secrets. Each instrument bore testament to the brutal truth of my profession – that beneath the veneer of civility, we are all animals, driven by a primal need for dominance and control.

As I zipped my bag closed, I allowed myself a moment of reflection, considering the path that lay before me. Ravenna, a city steeped in history and intrigue, would serve as the stage for our deadly dance – a labyrinth where secrets whispered through ancient alleyways and desire glinted like gold beneath the moonlit domes of Byzantine cathedrals.

I could feel the pull of temptation, a seductive force that beckoned me into the darkness, promising secrets and sins beyond my wildest imaginings. And yet, I knew that to succumb to such allurements would be to lose myself in their embrace, spiraling ever deeper into the abyss that lay at the heart of my own nature.

With a final glance around my apartment, I hefted the bag onto my shoulder and stepped out into the morning haze, my resolve firm and my senses honed to a razor's edge. The game was afoot, and I – Luigi Ferro, private investigator and master of deception – would emerge victorious.

I gave Caterina a heartfelt kiss on her red, soft lips before I swung my leg over my trusty Vespa. The familiar contours of its seat beneath me gave me comfort, and I revved the engine to life.

As I zipped through the streets of San Marino en route to Rimini, the wind caressed my face, teasing tendrils of hair free from their slicked-back restraint.

"Ravenna," I mused, my thoughts drifting to the ancient city that would be my destination. A place where history and desire intertwined in a sensual dance, its secrets lurking beneath the surface like the shimmering scales of a serpent coiled within the depths of the Adriatic Sea.

I could feel the pull of temptation, a siren's song that beckoned me onward, promising a world of intrigue and danger that would test my every skill and instinct. And yet, there was something more – a sense of purpose that ran deeper than mere curiosity or ambition.

*

As the train rumbled north through the morning, the sun rising over the sea seemed to wash away the sinister secrets of the night, like cutting through the tendrils of a creeping vine with a machete. But no matter how seductive the shadows may be, I knew that only through the ruthless pursuit of truth could I hope to unravel this web of darkness and bring justice to the tragic victim whose life had been so cruelly snuffed out.

The Ravenna train station, an elegant yet weathered edifice, greeted me with open arms as I disembarked into the crisp morning air. I was immediately struck by the contrast between the city's historical beauty and the grim nature of my visit. The old town welcomed me with its tree-lined streets and a wonderful spring sun.

"Signor Ferro?" A voice sliced through my reverie

like a dagger. I turned to see a man clad in a taxi driver's uniform, his dark eyes regarding me with a mixture of suspicion and curiosity.

"Si," I replied curtly, nodding towards my small overnight bag.

"The Umbri International School sent me," he stated, already placing my luggage into the trunk. I raised an eyebrow at his intuition but said nothing.

"How nice," I responded, sliding into the back seat of the cab. As we drove away from the station, I couldn't help but drink in the sensual dance of sunlight on the streets, the shadows flirting with the radiance of the morning light.

"Beautiful, isn't it?" the driver remarked, catching my gaze in the rearview mirror. "Such a shame about that girl, though."

"Indeed," I murmured, my thoughts turning inward as we approached the gates of the boarding school. My heart quickened, a potent mix of determination and apprehension coursing through my veins like liquid fire.

"Here we are, Signore," the driver announced, barely concealing his eagerness to be rid of me.

"Thank you," I muttered, handing him a few bills before stepping out of the vehicle. Breathing deeply, I paused for a moment to take in the imposing facade of the palatial school, its secrets hidden behind walls that had borne witness to centuries of history and desire.

"Buona fortuna," the driver called out before speeding away, his words echoing ominously in my ears. I knew that luck would play little part in what was to come; only skill, perseverance, and an unquenchable thirst for justice would lead me to the truth.

I strode towards the entrance of Umbri International School, every fiber of my being focused on the task ahead. A darkness lurked beneath the seductive beauty of Ravenna's architecture, waiting to ensnare me in its tangled web of deceit and corruption. And ensnared I would be, willingly, if it meant bringing her killer to light.

"Signor Ferro," Madame Merola's voice invaded my thoughts, her tone a seductive blend of urgency and vulnerability. "Follow me to my office."

As Madame Merola led me through the hallowed halls of the exclusive boarding school, my senses were immediately engaged in an unusual blend of old-world charm and modern sophistication. The air was perfumed with a subtle mix of beeswax, used for polishing the ancient wood, and a faint, floral fragrance, perhaps lingering from the gardens outside.

The corridors were lined with polished oak panels, each telling stories of generations past. My steps echoed on the marble floor, a rhythmic reminder of the school's enduring legacy. The walls were adorned with portraits of distinguished alumni and founders, their stern gazes following me as I passed as if evaluating my worthiness to tread these privileged grounds.

Occasional bursts of youthful energy punctuated the air from distant classrooms, the muffled sounds of education in progress. The blend of voices, some eager, some weary, added a layer of vitality to the otherwise solemn atmosphere.

As we progressed, I couldn't help but notice the meticulous attention to detail: the perfectly arranged flower vases, the impeccably polished brass fixtures, and the artfully arranged bookshelves that seemed to hold centuries of knowledge. The aroma of freshly brewed coffee wafted from a staff room, briefly pulling my thoughts away from the task at hand.

Finally, we reached Madame Merola's office. The heavy oak door creaked open to reveal a room that was a testament to her personality and position. Books lined the walls, a grand desk sat prominently, and large windows offered a view of the sprawling school grounds. The scent of leather from well-worn chairs mingled with a hint of her perfume, creating an ambiance of authority and elegance.

I stepped into her office, ready to unravel the mysteries that lay within these walls, aware that every corner of this place held secrets waiting to be discovered.

"Allow me to provide additional details about the tragic incident," she stared, indicating a chair for me to sit on.

I acquiesced, the lure of darkness too potent to resist. "Proceed, Madame."

"Her name was Alicia Hodler, born in Switzerland, coming from a very influential family," she said, her words sketching a picture of affluence and influence. "Well, most students come from such families," she shrugged and smiled. "Alicia was an outstanding student, held in high esteem by her classmates and educators, and her killing has left a shadow over the whole school."

I could almost see the beautiful, young Alicia, her golden hair cascading down her back like a waterfall of lustrous silk, a radiant smile adorning her lips as she navigated the hallowed ancient halls of Umbri International School.

"Such a tragedy," I murmured, the heady cocktail of desire and danger teasing at my senses. "How did the events unfold?"

"Her lifeless body was found in a narrow alley just outside the city center, her dress torn and bloodied, her once-vibrant eyes now clouded with the finality of death," Madame Merola's voice trembled, a soft sob escaping her. "She had gone out with friends from school, and they became separated during the course of the evening."

"Any leads? The police?" I queried, the taste of intrigue bittersweet upon my tongue. My fingers instinctively yearned for the soothing burn of gin, the twist of lime a tart reminder of the complexities this case would undoubtedly present.

"None, Signor Ferro. The local authorities are at a loss, and we fear for the safety of our other students," she admitted, a hint of desperation seeping into her voice.

I pondered on this revelation, my gaze drawn to the elegant curve of a passing woman's neck, the sensuous line of her collarbone exposed beneath a delicate shawl. The promise of power, the desire for control – these were the driving forces behind such a heinous act, and

I knew that in order to unravel the mystery of Alicia Hodler's death, I must first understand the darkest recesses of the human heart.

"Very well, Madame Merola," I finally acquiesced, sensing an irresistible challenge and compelled by the urgency in her voice. "I will have to see where she was found and talk to her closest friends and teachers. Do you have the name of the investigating Commissario?"

"Yes, of course," she sighed with relief. "His name is Commissario Ettora Scarpa. And I will put you in contact with all her friends and teachers. You don't know how much this means to us."

2

Madame Merola, my guide and matriarch of this esteemed institution, sauntered ahead of me. The sun cast golden rays onto her raven hair, shimmering with each graceful step she took.

"Signor Ferro," she purred, "Allow me to show you around our prestigious academy. I'm sure you'll find it quite...stimulating." Her lips curved into a secretive smile as she gestured toward the manicured gardens with a sweep of her slender arm.

We strolled over the open courtyard, past ancient olive and citrus trees that whispered in the breeze. Madame Merola regaled me with tales of the school's noble past, pointing out statues of illustrious alumni dressed in their finest robes, forever frozen in time. The weight of history hung heavy in the air, mingling with the scent of roses and intrigue.

As we approached the building with the living quarters, its ochre walls awash in the sun's warm embrace, Madame Merola led me inside to the room I'd call home during my investigation.

"I trust you will find our accommodations suitable, Signor Ferro," she said, her voice dripping with honeyed charm.

I stepped into the guest room, greeted by the seductive dance of sunlight filtering through billowing curtains. An inviting king-sized bed beckoned from the center of the room, adorned with silken sheets that rippled like the surface of a tranquil lake. A velvet chaise lounge stood by the window, offering a respite for contemplation and desire.

"Comfort and luxury are top priorities here at the academy," Madame Merola murmured, her eyes lingering on the plush pillows piled atop the bed. "Our guests and our students should not feel they miss anything during their stay with us. I trust you'll find everything you need and more within these walls."

"Indeed, Madame," I replied, my gaze drifting toward the window with its breathtaking view of the verdant grounds. "It's quite an impressive setting."

"Ah, but it's not just the accommodations that make our school so exceptional," she purred, leaning in close enough for me to catch a hint of mint on her breath. "The people here are just as intriguing, each with their own specialties and secrets."

"Secrets, you say?" I raised an eyebrow, curiosity piqued.

"Indeed, Signor Ferro," Madame Merola said with a wink. "But discovering them is half the fun, wouldn't you agree?"

"Maybe so," I mused, feeling the pull of temptation tugging at my resolve. "Though some secrets are more dangerous than others."

"But what's life without a little danger?" she replied, her eyes sparkling with mischief.

"Something far less interesting, I'd imagine," I conceded, allowing myself a small smile.

With a final smoldering glance, Madame Merola left me to settle in and explore the academy's secrets on my own. I opened the window of my room, letting the vibrant warmth of the sun into my bones as I contemplated my next move. A subtle scent of citrus and rosemary lingered in the air, caressing my senses like a lover's tender touch.

"Signor Ferro," a voice called out from the courtyard outside. A tall, slender boy in an impeccably tailored gray uniform, a crisp white shirt approached my window, his eyes gleaming with curiosity. "I'm Lorenzo, head of the student council. We heard you were here to investigate Alicia's murder."

"Indeed," I replied, taking note of the boy's obvious pride in his position.

"Perhaps I can introduce you to some of my fellow students?" he asked.

Of course, I accepted his invitation, and the next moment, we met in the corridor.

"It would help me if I could get a sense of the atmosphere around here," I said after our proper introductions. Lorenzo was Italian, one of just a handful, from a family of diplomats in Rome.

"Of course," he agreed, gesturing for me to follow him as we wove our way through clusters of eager young minds, their laughter ringing like crystal.

"Here we have Francesca and Giulia," Lorenzo said, indicating two girls in the school's uniform, their gazes sharp and assessing as they sized me up. "They're both top of their class in literature."

"Ah, the sirens of prose," I mused aloud, my gaze flitting between them like a restless moth. "Tell me, ladies, did Alicia share your passion for the written word?"

"Hardly," Francesca scoffed, her disdain palpable. "She was more interested in art, fashion, and parties than in anything truly intellectual."

"Though she did have a taste for poetry," Giulia added thoughtfully, a hint of melancholy etching itself across her features. "She often spoke of her fondness for Dante and Petrarch."

"Interesting," I murmured, filing away this tidbit like a jeweler selecting a rare gem. "And what of her friendships? Was she close to anyone in particular?"

"Besides Amber, you mean?" Lorenzo interjected before the girls could respond. "They were inseparable. But Alicia was friendly with most people – she had a way of making everyone feel special."

"Yet not all friendships are created equal, Signore," Francesca pointed out, her eyes narrowing as she observed my reaction.

"Indeed," I agreed, feeling the weight of unspoken truths in her words. "Thank you for your insights. I'll be sure to keep them in mind."

As we continued our tour of the courtyard, I studied the subtle ballet of glances and gestures that played out among the students, revealing hidden alliances and simmering rivalries. It was a dance of desire and power, each step calculated to advance or undermine, and I knew that somewhere within its intricate choreography lay the key to unlocking Alicia's tragic fate.

"Signor Ferro," Lorenzo called, pulling me from

my thoughts. "There's one other person I think you should meet."

He gestured towards a cluster of students near the fountain, their laughter tinkling like the delicate notes of a forgotten melody. Among them, I noticed a young man whose demeanor was a stark contrast to the others – his eyes darted nervously, sweat glistening on his brow like morning dew on fresh roses. Intrigued, I followed Lorenzo through the throng, the rich scent of mingling perfumes enveloping me like a lover's embrace.

"Marco," Lorenzo addressed the jittery youth, who visibly flinched at the sound of his name. "This is Signor Ferro, the investigator looking into Alicia's death."

"Ah, y–yes," Marco stammered, his gaze flickering between me and the ground, unable to hold either for long. "I'm sorry about what happened to her. She was... she was a good friend."

"Indeed," I replied, carefully watching the youths every move. "Tell me, Marco, did you notice anything... unusual in the days leading up to her death?"

"Unusual?" he echoed, nervously fidgeting with the cuff of his tailored shirt. "No, not really; I mean, we all have our secrets, don't we? But nothing that would lead to... to this."

"Secrets, you say?" I probed, my curiosity piqued like the whisper of silk against skin. "Did Alicia have any secrets that you're aware of?"

"Everyone has secrets, Signore," Marco said evasively, his eyes darting to the side. "It's only natural."

"Perhaps," I conceded, my senses sharpened by the

intoxicating blend of desire and danger that hung thick in the air. "But some secrets are more dangerous than others, wouldn't you agree?"

"Signore, I really must be going – class," Marco blurted, his face flushed with a mixture of fear and guilt.

"Of course," I replied, stepping back to let him pass. As he hurried away, I couldn't help but wonder what dark truths lay buried beneath his nervous facade.

"Interesting fellow," Lorenzo mused, watching Marco's retreating figure. "Seems like he's carrying quite a burden on those slender shoulders."

I nodded in agreement, my thoughts turning once more to the labyrinthine web of secrets and desires that had ensnared us all. "But aren't we all, Lorenzo? Aren't we all?"

*

Madame Merola invited me to join the teachers at their table for lunch. I found my seat next to a statuesque woman with hair the color of midnight. She introduced herself as Natalia, the history teacher, her words laced with a passion for the past that surpassed mere academic interest. "Signore, I hope you'll find our school's storied past as fascinating as I do."

"History can reveal much about the present," I noted, intrigued by her fervor. "And perhaps even offer clues to the future."

"True," she conceded, her eyes narrowing as if measuring my worth. "But only to those who possess the insight to see beneath the surface of things."

"An astute observation," I replied, feeling the weight of her scrutiny. "One that I shall keep in mind as I navigate the labyrinth of secrets that await me."

"Thank you," she murmured, her gaze lingering on me like a velvet caress. "For knowledge is power, Signor Ferro, and with power comes the ability to shape the world as we see fit."

"Indeed, Signora," I agreed, my thoughts returning to the task at hand – piecing together the tangled web of desire, ambition, and deceit that lay hidden within the academy's elegant facade.

A young woman who seemed to glide through the food hall like a specter clothed in silk and lace approached us and sat down on my other side. Her name was Gloria, the gymnastics instructor. Her lithe form a living testament to the power of graceful movement.

"Signor Ferro," she greeted, her voice a sultry purr. "I've heard such intriguing things about you. Do tell me, what do you hope to find in our hallowed halls?"

"The past, Signorina," I answered, my gaze locked with hers. "A past that will uncover the hidden truths that dwell within these walls."

"Then you'll have a lot to do," she promised, her eyes smoldering with an untamed fire. "But beware, for not everything is as it seems, and some doors are best left unopened."

"Sound advice," I conceded, though I knew I was never one to shy away from danger's seductive embrace. "But sometimes, the allure of the unknown is too powerful to resist."

"Indeed," she agreed, her lips curving into a secretive smile before she drifted away, leaving me to ponder the enigma that she presented.

The school's head chef entered and presented the three-course luncheon: "Today we are pleased to offer you a start of Minestrone Soup, followed by a Fusion Pasta with Chicken Alfredo, and ending with a Panna Cotta with Mixed Berry Compote." He made a somewhat overdramatic pause to let the presentation sink in. "As usual, you'll find carafes of Iced Herbal Tea and Water."

The students applauded, more of obligation and politeness than genuine appreciation.

The warm aroma of the Minestrone soup filled the grand food hall, its steam rising gently from the bowl. I took a spoonful, savoring the rich blend of vegetables and herbs, each ingredient perfectly harmonious. The soup was comforting, like a gentle reminder of home.

Around me, the bustling hall was a blend of modern efficiency and old-world charm. The staff, clad in crisp uniforms, moved with practiced grace, attending to each student with a smile. I admired their seamless coordination, a dance of hospitality that made the large space feel intimate.

My main course, the Chicken Alfredo Pasta, was a delightful fusion. The creamy sauce was indulgent yet not overwhelming, and the grilled chicken added just the right amount of savory depth. The side of sautéed vegetables was a vibrant addition, their slight crunch a pleasant contrast.

As I enjoyed the meal, I exchanged light

conversation with my tablemates. We shared stories from our morning classes and plans for the weekend, the laughter mingling with the clinking of cutlery.

Dessert was a splendid finale. The Panna Cotta, adorned with berry compote, was a testament to the art of simplicity. Its delicate flavor and silky texture were a perfect end to the meal, leaving me content and full of energy for the rest of the day.

"Signor Ferro," Madame Merola purred as we left the table, her voice as smooth as the pearls that adorned her slender neck." Allow me to introduce you to our esteemed art teacher, Signora Miriam Petrilla."

I looked at the woman at her side – a vision of feminine grace wrapped in hues of crimson and gold. Her attire, like the brushstrokes of a Renaissance master, clung to her lithe form with sensuous abandon. The corners of her full lips curved upward in a smile that promised both pleasure and pain.

"Signora Petrilla," I murmured, my gaze lingering on the delicate curve of her neck as I took her proffered hand. "A pleasure to make your acquaintance."

"Likewise, Signor Ferro," she replied, her dark eyes gleaming with a tantalizing hint of secrets yet to be revealed. "We are all so pleased you could take on our terrible problem…"

"No problem, Signora," I said, releasing her hand reluctantly. "I've understood that this is a very delicate matter."

"Miriam has a unique gift," Madame Merola interjected, her tone laced with admiration. "Not only for creating exquisite works of art but also for drawing out the hidden talents of our young charges."

"Indeed?" I raised an eyebrow, intrigued by both the woman herself and her apparent ability to shape the raw clay of youth into something rare and beautiful. "That is quite the skill, Signora."

"Art," Miriam replied, her voice a sultry whisper that caressed my ears like velvet, "is a window to the soul, Signor Ferro. To see it through the eyes of another is to glimpse their innermost desires – and perhaps even their darkest secrets."

"Would you care to give me a tour of your studio, Signora?" I inquired, sensing that there might be more to this woman than met the eye. "I confess a keen interest in the creative process and would welcome the opportunity to learn from a master such as yourself."

"Of course," she answered, the enigmatic smile returning to her lips. "It would be my pleasure, Signor Ferro."

As we moved through the halls, our footsteps echoing off the polished stone, I knew that I had entered a world of temptation and desire – a place where the line between art and life blurred into an intoxicating haze of beauty and power. And at the heart of it all stood Miriam Petrilla, her allure, a seductive force that threatened to ensnare me in its silken web.

"Be careful, Signor Ferro," she warned, her gaze locked with mine as we stood on the threshold of her sanctuary. "Once you have tasted the forbidden fruit, there can be no turning back."

"Thank you for the warning, Signora," I replied,

my pulse quickening at the promise of what lay ahead. "But I have never been one to shy away from danger or desire."

"Then you are in good company, Signor Ferro," she whispered, her smile both inviting and deadly. "For in my world, they are one and the same."

As I stepped into the school's art studio with Miriam Petrilla, the space felt like a sanctuary of creativity. The walls were adorned with an array of student artworks, each telling its unique story. With her graceful and almost poetic movements, Miriam guided me through the room. The way her long skirt swayed gently with each step, complementing her slender figure, added an artistic flair to her presence.

"There's a story behind each piece," she said softly, her fingers lightly tracing the edge of a canvas as we passed by. "You can almost read the artist's state of mind through their brushstrokes."

Her observations were insightful, revealing a depth of understanding not just of art but of the human psyche. Each artwork we paused at reflected a spectrum of emotions, from the chaotic swirls representing turmoil to the gentle hues of a peaceful landscape.

As we meandered through the studio, Miriam's passion for art and teaching was evident in her every word and gesture. She moved with a confidence that was both inspiring and captivating.

Finally, we stopped in front of a painting that immediately drew my attention. It depicted a serene twilight scene, the colors blending seamlessly, evoking a sense of calm and introspection.

"This is Alicia's work," Miriam said, her voice filled with a mix of pride and a subtle hint of sadness. "She has…had an incredible talent for capturing emotions. This piece… it's like she poured her soul into it."

I studied the painting, mesmerized by the way the brushstrokes conveyed not just the scene but the emotion behind it. Alicia, I knew, was an art major who had left an indelible mark on the department.

"Her skill was remarkable," I murmured, feeling a sense of loss for a fellow artist whose presence still lingered in the strokes of her masterpiece.

At that moment, surrounded by the legacy of students like Alicia, the art studio felt like a place where time stood still, preserving the essence of each artist who had found their voice within its walls.

With a final lingering glance at the enigmatic Miriam Petrilla, I left the art studio and headed back toward the dorms to visit Alicia's room.

I found myself in the dorm room once shared by Amber Boyd-Cohen and the late Alicia Hodler. The room was cast in a sultry half-light, courtesy of the Venetian blinds that graced the window, their slats angled just so to admit the golden beams of the setting sun. The setting was a blend of personal touches and institutional furnishings.

As the door clicked shut behind me, I began to scrutinize my surroundings, seeking to unravel the enigma of the slain Swiss beauty through the intimate details of her personal space.

I moved first to the desk, its polished surface scattered with an array of objects that hinted at a complex inner life: a well-thumbed copy of Dante's Inferno, a silver fountain pen engraved with her initials, a half-empty bottle of Chanel No. 5. Each item whispered tantalizingly of an existence both privileged and passionate, a heady cocktail of desire and ambition that had perhaps proved too potent for some.

"What dreams and fears did you harbor within this hallowed chamber, Alicia?" I mused, my fingers tracing the embossed cover of the book as if to divine the secrets it held.

Next, I turned my attention to the wardrobe, a towering antique of carved walnut that seemed to promise a treasure trove of sartorial revelations. Sliding the doors open, I found myself confronted by a veritable cornucopia of garments, each one more sumptuous than the last.

"Quite the collection," I murmured, running my hand over the silken fabric of a crimson dress, feeling the softness under my fingers. "And yet, I suspect there is more to you than meets the eye."

Suddenly, the door swung open, and Amber Boyd-Cohen, clad in the school's uniform, walked in. The gray cardigan neatly layered over a crisp white shirt, the tie knotted just so, her short pleated, blue skirt paired with white knee-high socks and sneakers. She carried the uniform with an air of nonchalant elegance, a stark contrast to the somber reason behind my visit.

She cocked her head, the blonde ponytail almost whipping against her back. Her brown eyes regarded me with a dismissive glance, her posture radiating indifference. "Can I help you?" she asked, her tone edged with impatience. It was clear she saw me as an unwelcome intrusion into her private space.

I introduced myself, "I'm Luigi Ferro, a private investigator looking into Alicia's death."

The ice in her eyes melted into a gentle stream of curiosity, softening her expression into something unexpectedly approachable.

"I need to get ready for gym class," she said, an undercurrent of urgency in her voice. Without a second thought, she began to undress right there in front of me. I turned my back, respecting her privacy, but I couldn't help but be taken aback by her nonchalant attitude. Her actions spoke of comfort with herself and her surroundings, a trait I found both intriguing and unusual in someone her age.

As I focused on the room's details, trying to uncover anything that might help my investigation, I heard the rustle of clothing and the occasional clink of a belt or zipper. Amber's voice floated over to me. "You really think you can find out who did this to Alicia?" she asked a hint of vulnerability in her voice now.

"I'm going to try my best," I replied, turning to face her, now dressed in figure-hugging leggings accentuating her curvy body and a colorful sports bra that barely managed to cover her large bosom. "Every detail helps. Sometimes, it's the smallest piece that completes the puzzle."

She nodded, her eyes reflecting a mix of emotions – fear, sadness, perhaps even a relief that someone was taking the case seriously.

Before she left, Amber paused at the door, looking

back at me. "Alicia didn't deserve what happened to her," she said softly, then hurried out, leaving me alone with my thoughts and the silent echoes of a room once filled with the vibrant energy of two young women, now halved by tragedy.

I took a deep breath, refocusing on the task at hand. Every student, every teacher, and every interaction in this school could be a vital clue. As I sifted through Alicia's belongings, I knew I had to remain objective, observant, and prepared for whatever secrets lay hidden within these walls. Amber, like everyone else in this school, was a piece of the puzzle – a puzzle I was determined to solve.

3

The sharp rap at my door cleaved through my dreams of the night like a stiletto slipping effortlessly between ribs. I was awake in an instant, the aftertaste of a good night's sleep lingering on my tongue. When the door creaked open, she was there—Amber Boyd-Cohen, an enigma swathed in the innocence of a schoolgirl's attire. But the uniform was a facade, her tie absent, and the white shirt undone to reveal the lacy underpinnings of seduction.

"Signor Ferro," she purred, her voice a velvet caress against the backdrop of my sparsely furnished room. The moonlight spilled across her curves, casting a chiaroscuro that played upon my senses.

"Miss Boyd-Cohen," I rasped, my words as rough as the stubble on my chin. "This is hardly appropriate."

"Appropriate is such a... subjective term, don't you think?" Her eyes glinted with mischief, brown orbs that held within them the depth of the Adriatic.

I shifted uncomfortably, feeling the weight of her gaze upon me like the heat of the Mediterranean sun. She stepped closer, the scent of her perfume mingling with the tang of my aftershave, which lingered on my clothes.

"Romero Salvini," she said, shifting the topic as if it were as easy as shedding layers—which in her case, seemed imminent. "He's Alicia's secret love, or so she thought." A scornful laugh escaped her lips, a sound that held more darkness than mirth. "But Romero, he's just a looser, crawling through the gutters of Ravenna."

"And why confide in me now?" I queried, my mind thrumming with suspicion, even as my body reacted to her proximity.

"Because," Amber leaned in, her breath hot upon my ear, "I'm attracted to real men, like you, Signor Ferro."

"Attraction can be a dangerous thing," I warned, knowing full well the treacherous path her words were paving.

"Only if one fears the flames," she retorted, her fingers dancing along the hem of her skirt—a provocative invitation.

"Listen, kid," I began, my resistance firming up like the cobblestones lining our ancient streets, "It's not appropriate for me to consort with students."

"Who's talking about consorting?" Amber teased, a coy smile playing on her lips. "I'm well versed in certain arts. Not the kind Alicia cared for—I indulge in the arts of erotica and sensualism." She took another calculated step, closing the gap between temptation and prudence.

"Amber—" My protest was cut short by her finger pressed against my lips.

"I'm of legal age, Luigi. And I can accommodate your every wish," she whispered, her words a siren song meant to crash willpower against the rocks.

"Age isn't the issue," I managed to say, pulling away from her touch. A wave of relief washed over me as I reclaimed some semblance of control. "It's about what's right."

"Right and wrong are merely threads in the tapestry of life, easily tangled, easily pulled," she countered, her confidence unshaken as she pressed her body against mine.

"Maybe so," I conceded, my thoughts racing to piece together this new revelation regarding Alicia and Romero. "But some threads are better left untouched."

With a sigh that spoke volumes of her thwarted intent, Amber took a step back, the moment of temptation dissipating like mist in the sunrise. "As you wish, Detective Ferro."

"Have a good day, Miss Boyd-Cohen," I said sternly, ushering her towards the door. As it clicked shut behind her, I was left alone with the ghostly echoes of desire and the intricate puzzle of a murder that was proving to be far more complex than I had anticipated.

The dawn was a shy onlooker, peering through drawn curtains and cracks in the walls, as I started a round of morning interviews.

"Signorina Vittoria," I greeted the young woman as she opened her dorm room door. She was a close confidant of Alicia Hodler. "I appreciate you seeing me this early."

"Anything for Alicia," she replied, her voice a tremulous note amidst the silence of the room. Her eyes, dewy with unspent grief, searched mine, seeking an ally or perhaps an avenger.

With the precision of a maestro conducting a requiem, I began our interview. "You were intimate with her secrets, were you not?"

"Of course," Vittoria whispered, her fingers

nervously fiddling with the hem of her pleated skirt. "We shared everything... or so I thought."

"Romero Salvini," I probed further, watching her reaction closely.

A subtle shift in demeanor, the tightening of her jaw—I caught it all. "He was a mistake," she hissed, a serpent's warning. "Alicia deserved better."

"Yet she chose him," I mused aloud, tapping into the reservoir of my interior thoughts, where suspicion swam like dark fish beneath the surface.

"They say that love is blind." Vittoria's laugh was devoid of humor, a hollow echo in the chamber of her loss.

"Or perhaps love is the veil that cloaks our true desires," I suggested, allowing the words to hang between us, a tapestry of implication.

The conversation flowed like a tangled web, each thread leading to more revelations. As the time wore on, Alicia's once innocent image began to unravel, revealing hidden depths and dark desires.

Vittoria spoke of secret rendezvous with powerful men, whispered about meetings in society's elite. She painted a picture of Alicia as an enigma, luring others into her seductive web with her charm and charisma. But as she delved deeper into Alicia's tales, hints of guilt and shame seeped out, regrets that she had not intervened.

I listened intently, my curiosity piqued by this complex young woman who seemed equal parts alluring and dangerous. In that dimly lit dorm room, Vittoria's words wove a spell over me, drawing me further down the rabbit hole of Alicia's twisted past.

"Thank you, Signorina," I said finally, closing the notebook which had become the repository of our dialogue. "You've been most helpful."

"Will you find who did this to her?" Vittoria asked, her gaze imploring me for a promise I wasn't sure I could keep.

"I plan to," I assured her, my tone as firm as the resolve hardening within me.

After I closed her door behind me, I stood alone, the ghost of Amber's seduction lingering like a question mark over the day's endeavors. The siren call of desire still pulsed in my veins, but now it was tempered by the urgency of the hunt—a predator's focus that would not be deterred by flesh or fantasy.

"Signor Ferro!" The voice came from the stairs where a student hastily approached me. Her cheeks were flushed, either from the climb or from the urgency of her message. "I thought you should know—Romero, he's not been seen. Since Alicia... since she..." She trailed off, biting her lip.

"Since she was taken from us," I finished for her. "Thank you. What's your name?"

"It's Margherita, Signore." She lowered her gaze and curtsied.

"Margherita," I said, catching her gaze. "If Romero surfaces, let me know."

"Of course. He used to work at a café not far from here – Romero that is." She glanced around nervously, as though afraid our conversation might summon specters from the hallowed texts surrounding us.

*

The moment I stepped out of the elite boarding school, the air of Ravenna greeted me with a blend of past and present. The city, with its mosaic of history and modernity, seemed to hum a tune that resonated with my current quest – the search for Romero, a crucial piece in the intricate puzzle of Alicia's murder.

Walking through the cobbled streets, the scent of fresh espresso and the rustic aroma of baked focaccia wafted from the quaint cafes lining the pathways. The city, steeped in history, stood as a testament to time – its ancient buildings a stark contrast to the lively chatter and the hustle of everyday life.

People moved about their day, some leisurely strolling with gelato in hand, others rushing through, a blur against the backdrop of timeless architecture. I couldn't help but think about how life's pace varied, how some could afford the leisure of a slow day while others, like Romero, might find themselves entangled in situations beyond their control.

As I navigated through the narrow streets, the grandeur of Ravenna's Byzantine mosaics and the solemnity of its ancient churches gave way to the more modest parts of town. Here, the buildings bore the weight of years less gracefully, and the faces I passed seemed etched with stories not so different from the one I was chasing.

My thoughts were a tangled web. Romero, the

missing link, was last seen working at a small café, according to the murmurs within the school. But since Alicia's murder, he had vanished, like a ghost slipping through the cracks of the city.

Finally, I reached the café where Romero was said to work. It was a modest establishment, nestled between a bookshop and a florist, its sign weathered but welcoming. The aroma of strong coffee hit me as I stepped inside, the scent mingling with the faint smell of old books and wilting flowers from its neighbors.

The café was a cozy haven, a stark contrast to the grandiosity I had left behind at the school. It was filled with an eclectic mix of patrons – some immersed in their books, others engaged in hushed conversations. The walls were lined with photographs of Ravenna, capturing moments of its history and the daily life of its people.

I approached the counter, where an elderly man with a friendly smile took my order. As I waited for my coffee, I casually inquired about Romero. The man's smile faltered for a moment, a shadow crossing his face. "Romero? Haven't seen him since... well, for a few days. Youths you know – can't be trusted."

The café suddenly felt smaller, the air heavier. It was as if Romero's absence had left a void even in this humble corner of the city. I took my coffee and found an empty seat outside, watching the world outside continue its dance, oblivious to the drama unfolding in its midst.

Sipping the bitter coffee, my mind raced. Where had Romero gone? Was he in hiding, or something worse? Alicia's death had sent ripples through this city, disturbing the surface of many lives. I knew then that finding Romero was key – not just for the case, but to understand the broader picture that was slowly coming into focus.

In this city of ancient secrets and living stories, I felt the weight of my task. But as I sat in that small café, the pieces of the puzzle beckoning, I was determined to uncover the truth, no matter where it led.

The small piazza was busy with locals and tourists alike. An elderly man, properly dressed in a three piece suit and bowtie crossed the square and entered the bookshop next door. Two ladies were picking our flowers, chatting gayly, at my other side.

"Signor Ferro," a girl in the school's uniform greeted me, stepping cautiously closer. Her hair like the raven's wing and her smile tight as the strings of a violin. Her name was Valentina, a close friend of the victim, or so she claimed.

"Yes," I said, my tone brooking no argument, gesturing for her to sit across from me. She slid into the chair, her movements deliberate, each gesture practiced, perhaps even performed.

"Everyone thought Alicia had eyes only for Romero," Valentina began, the words slipping from her lips like silk. "But there were others... admirers who lurked in the shadows, yearning for her…pleasures…"

"Names," I demanded, the flavor of command rich on my tongue.

"Giorgio, Luca… Even Professor Marini, though he'd

never admit it." Her voice dropped to a conspiratorial murmur.

"Accusations without evidence are mere fancies, ragazza." I leaned back, studying her through narrowed eyes. It was a dance, and she was leading now, but I knew the steps all too well.

"Perhaps," she conceded with a shrug that lifted her shoulders in a way that seemed rehearsed. "But eyes see more than they tell."

"Indeed." I let the word hang between us, heavy with implication. There was something she wasn't saying—a secret held close like a hand of cards.

"Signor Ferro," she said, voice low, "you seek truth in a web of lies. Be careful not to become entangled." With that, she rose, leaving me amidst the clatter of cups and the bitter aroma of coffee grounds.

I sat there, surrounded by the ambient sounds of life continuing unabated, contemplating her words. The new information necessitated a mental realignment— the victim's life was not a straight line but rather a nexus of intersecting paths, each with its own hidden destination.

"Valentina!" I called out before she could disappear. She paused, a silhouette against the light spilling down from the morning sky.

"Those names you mentioned..." I trailed off, watching as her back stiffened. "They're just part of the scenery, aren't they?"

"Scenery can be telling, Signor Ferro," she said, turning around. "It sets the stage for what's to come."

"Or distracts from what is already there," I countered, my mind racing through the possibilities, a predator.

Valentina disappeared in the colorful crowd, and I sat there for a moment longer, lost in thought. The information she had dropped was like a piece in a puzzle that didn't fit until you looked at it from an entirely new angle.

I tossed back the last of my espresso, feeling the caffeine hit my veins with a welcome jolt. It was time to act. Rising from my seat, I threw down a few euros and stepped into the streets of Ravenna.

The rest of the day yielded little but frustration. Romero remained elusive, a phantom cloaked in rumors and half-truths. The town seemed to conspire in silence, a community bound by unspoken pacts. Students whispered and glanced away as I approached, their eyes sliding off me like rain on slick cobblestones.

I retired to my guest room and laid out the interview transcripts. Something gnawed at me—a sense of deception that clung to the pages like perfume to skin. One student, in particular, caught my attention.

"Luca," I said, tapping the transcript bearing his name. His story was too clean, a path swept free of debris. I could almost see him sitting across from me, the twitch in his jaw when he spoke of the victim, the way his eyes darted to the door.

"What are you hiding?" The question was a whisper in the growing darkness of the room. I leaned back in my chair, fingers steepled before me.

"Desire, temptation, power..." I mused aloud, the themes of this case weaving through my thoughts like threads in a tapestry. The students sought to seduce me with their words, to cloak their motives in layers of silk and charm. But beneath the finery lay bare flesh and bone—raw, unvarnished truth.

A discreet knock on my door interrupted my brooding.

Miriam Petrilla, the school's discreet art teacher, stood outside. Her entrance was like a brushstroke on a blank canvas, transforming the mundane into something intriguing.

She was a striking figure, brunette, with hair cascading in loose waves that framed her face, a face that held an intelligent, inquisitive look. She was in her 30s, but there was a timeless quality about her, something that defied easy categorization. Her slim, attractive figure was accentuated by her choice of clothing – simple yet stylish, with an artistic flair that made her stand out.

She moved with a grace that was almost hypnotic, each step measured and deliberate. There was an air of confidence about her, a quiet assurance that she carried effortlessly. As she approached, I couldn't help but be drawn to her, her presence filling the room with an undeniable allure.

"Signor Ferro," she said, her voice smooth and melodic, "have you had any progress with Alicia's case?" Her eyes locked onto mine, a depth of emotion swirling within them, reflecting a mixture of curiosity and something akin to a challenge.

She took a seat across from me, crossing her legs in a way that was both casual and purposefully seductive.

Her long dress parted along the shapely, slim leg and she absently dangled her sandal from the dainty foot. There was an elegance to her movements, a sense of purpose in every gesture. It was as if she was painting her own portrait with each motion, creating an image of poise and intrigue.

"Everything in the case is not about Alicia," I replied, letting my gase caress her figure from the perfectly painted red toenails, over the curve of her slim legs to the enigmatic brown eyes. She held my gaze, allowing me to explore their depths further. They were pools of knowing, reflecting secrets yet untold.

"Poor Alicia," she began, her words heavy with a sorrow that was not entirely her own. "She was more entangled in the lives of others than anyone realized."

"Entangled how?" I prodded, watching as she poured us each a glass of amber liquid that glowed like a captured sunset.

"Romances are common among students, but hers... it was different." She paused, leaning forward before she continued. "She knew things about certain individuals. Things that could ruin reputations."

"Things worth killing over?" My question hung between us like a blade poised to fall.

"Maybe?" she shrugged, her lips curled into an enigmatic smile.

As we talked, I found myself momentarily distracted by the way she bit her lip when deep in thought, or how her eyes seemed to dance with amusement at certain topics. She was fully aware of her effect, using her sensuality as a tool, both to distract and to probe.

Miriam Petrilla was not just an art teacher; she was an artwork herself, a living, breathing embodiment of aesthetic and mystery. As she spoke about Alicia, her expressions shifted between sorrow, anger, and a hint of something else – a complexity that I couldn't quite grasp.

I knew I had to tread carefully. In the world of elite boarding schools and hidden secrets, Miriam Petrilla was a captivating enigma, a puzzle within the larger mystery I was trying to solve. Her allure was undeniable, but so was the intelligence and depth she masked behind those artful smiles and calculated glances.

The sun was setting over the roof as we rose, coming to stand very close to each other.

"I'm sure you'll find the truth," she whispered. "But in Ravenna, the truth has many shadows."

"Shadows can be illuminated," I countered, savoring her hot breath at my cheek.

"Be cautious, detective," she warned, her fingers briefly brushing mine. "Some shadows bite back when cornered."

As she left the room, a part of her essence lingered, like the afterglow of a sunset. The encounter had left me with more questions than answers, but one thing was certain – Miriam Petrilla was a force to be reckoned with, and whatever her role in this intricate web was, I intended to see more of her.

*

The sun was a low-hanging fruit, ripe and heavy in the sky, casting amber hues across the cobblestones of the city. I found myself wandering this maze of history, where every street corner whispered tales of ancient amours and bloodied vendettas.

"Signor Ferro," came a voice, laced with a melody that could only belong to youth.

I turned to find Amber Boyd-Cohen leaning against the flaking plaster wall of an old trattoria. The afternoon light caught the edges of her blonde ponytail like a halo, but the darkness in her eyes spoke of a different kind of sanctity.

"Miss Boyd-Cohen," I acknowledged, my tone neutral, though my senses were already picking up the faint scent of jasmine from her skin.

"Taking a stroll?" she asked, her question as casual as her pose, one leg bent at the knee, the heel of her school shoe scuffing the stone.

"More of a hunt," I replied. "For truth."

"Ah, la verità—such a slippery lover," she teased, pushing away from the wall, her movements fluid and full of intention.

"Indeed. And what brings you here, Signorina?" I inquired, focusing on the play of shadows across her face rather than the curves that her clothes did little to conceal. Now dressed in figure hugging denims and a well tailored jacket over a black bra.

"Looking for a friend," she said, her tone suddenly somber.

"Or perhaps following someone?"

Her lips quirked up at that. "Maybe I'm following you, Detective. You're a hard man to keep track of."

"Yet, you seem adept at it." My gaze narrowed slightly, trying to decipher the game she was playing.

"Maybe I have my reasons."

"Such as?" I pressed, my instincts tingling like live wires.

She stepped closer, close enough that I could see the delicate lace covering her bosoms. "I know things," she murmured, her breath a warm whisper against my cheek. "About Alicia... and Romero."

"Romero Salvini," I uttered the name, watching her reaction closely. "What about him?"

"Let's just say, he's not the saint everyone thinks he is." She reached out, her fingertips grazing my forearm. "I've seen them together, you know. Alicia thought she was good at hiding her secrets, but not from me."

"Are you confessing to something more than curiosity, Amber?" I asked, my voice a low growl of suspicion.

"Me? Oh no," she breathed out a soft chuckle. "But when you dance with the devil, someone's bound to get burned."

"Is that a threat?" I questioned, the air between us charged with an energy that was both dangerous and enticing.

"No, Detective. It's an invitation." Her gaze held mine, unwavering and bold.

"An invitation to what exactly?"

"To explore the depths of this mystery together," she said, her voice dropping to a conspiratorial hush. "I can show you the hidden paths, the secret rendezvous spots. But are you brave enough to follow?"

"Bravery isn't the issue—it's a question of propriety." I stepped back, reclaiming the space between us.

"Propriety is just another cage, Signor Ferro," she retorted, her eyes flashing with defiance.

"Perhaps," I allowed, my mind churning through the implications of her words. "But even a caged bird can sing of freedom—and truth."

"Then listen," she started. "Romero and Alicia, they sometimes hung out at an old industrial building, on the outskirts," she whispered, her voice laced with a mix of fear and seduction.

"Do you have the address?" This was the break I needed.

"I know where it is, and I'm going to show you," she smiled, taking my hand and pulling me forward.

I walked, my thoughts a jumble of possibilities and dead ends. The industrial area wasn't a place for the faint-hearted, a stark contrast to the sheltered lives of the boarding school students. What were Alicia and Romero seeking in such a place? A refuge from prying eyes, or something more sinister?

The further we ventured from the city center, the more the scenery changed. The quaint cafes and bustling shops gave way to quieter streets, the architecture growing older, more worn. The air held a different scent here – less of espresso and more of the earth, mixed with a hint of the sea.

We passed by locals who looked at us with a mixture of curiosity and indifference. A private investigator in his prime walking alongside a blonde beauty who liked to show it off, but in a town like Ravenna, not much seemed to surprise its inhabitants anymore.

The buildings grew sparse as I approached the industrial outskirts. Here, the remnants of Ravenna's manufacturing past stood like silent sentinels, their empty windows staring back at me. Suddenly Amber tugged my arm and nodded towards an old industrial building, its dilapidated structure a skeleton of its former glory.

"You'd better wait here," I told her, and for once she didn't protest.

Approaching the building, I felt a chill that had little to do with the evening breeze. The walls, streaked with grime and graffiti, told stories of abandonment. Broken glass crunched under my feet as we stepped inside, the echo of my footsteps a stark reminder of the building's emptiness.

The interior was vast, a cavernous space once alive with the sounds of machinery and workers. Now, it stood silent, save for the occasional drip of water from the leaky roof. Shafts of dying light pierced through the broken panes, casting long shadows.

I moved carefully, my senses heightened. Each step took me deeper into the building's belly, where Alicia and Romero had once sought solace. I could almost picture them here, two figures against the backdrop of decay, their laughter a brief respite from the expectations of their worlds.

The place was a maze of corridors and rooms, each turn revealing more of its forsaken state. Old equipment lay scattered, rusted and forgotten. Graffiti adorned the walls, the work of those who briefly claimed this place as their own.

But of Romero, there was no sign. The building, for all its secrets, remained silent on his whereabouts. I left as the sun dipped below the horizon, the building once again succumbing to the shadows of the night.

As I turned to leave, a glimmer of something outside caught my eye. A shed, tucked away in the back of the property, seemingly insignificant yet oddly out of place in this graveyard of industry. My curiosity piqued, I made my way towards it.

The shed stood alone, its wooden frame weathered by time and elements. The door was slightly ajar, creaking mournfully as I pushed it open. Inside, the air was damp and heavy, filled with the musty scent of mold and the earthy aroma of rotting wood. Faint shafts of light pierced through the cracks in the walls, casting long, ghostly shadows. The shed was cluttered with relics of the past – rusted tools, broken furniture, and piles of old newspapers, creating a mausoleum of memories.

In the far corner, shrouded in shadows, sat a hulking figure. The man before me bore little resemblance to the vibrant individual described by those who knew Romero. Gaunt, his skin ashen and gray, his once robust frame now thin and frail, he seemed a mere shell of his former self.

As I approached, his eyes flickered with a mix of fear and recognition. "Who are you? What do you want?" he croaked, his voice barely above a whisper.

"Romero, I am trying to discover what happened to Alicia," I said, my voice soft but firm.

"I didn't kill her, Signore. I loved her," Romero sobbed, his body shaking with each word. "I never wanted any of this to happen."

I looked at him, seeing not just a witness or a suspect, but a human being consumed by grief and fear. "I believe you, Romero," I said gently. "But you need to tell me what you know."

He shuddered, pulling his threadbare coat tighter around him. Tears began to well up in his eyes as he recounted the fateful night.

"I left her a few blocks from the school," he began, his voice trembling. "We had to keep our meetings secret. She was scared that night, said she felt like we were being watched."

His words hung in the damp air, a tangible presence in the cramped space.

"Then I heard it," he continued, a note of horror creeping into his voice. "A loud shot, echoing between the buildings. It was so sudden, so... final." He paused, choking on his words.

I leaned in closer, urging him to go on. "Did you see anything else?"

Romero nodded, wiping his eyes with a dirty sleeve. "A car," he whispered. "A black Mercedes. It sped away right after the shot. I was scared, Signor Ferro. I didn't know what to do. I ran."

4

The first light of dawn was creeping through the curtains as I stirred awake in the guest room of the boarding school. For a moment, I lay there, the weight of the previous night's revelations pressing heavily upon my mind. Finding Romero and ensuring his safety had been a small victory in this complex web of secrets and lies, yet it was a victory nonetheless.

I stretched, feeling the stiffness in my muscles, a physical reminder of the night's exertions. The satisfaction of having located Romero, who had been living in fear and seclusion since Alicia's death, was palpable. There was a sense of relief in returning him to the safety of his own home, a small beacon of hope in the shadow of tragedy.

My thoughts drifted back to what he had told me, his voice trembling with fear and uncertainty. The sound of a loud shot echoed through the streets of Ravenna, followed by the sight of a black Mercedes speeding away. These details painted a sinister picture, hinting at something much larger and more dangerous than a mere lovers' rendezvous gone wrong.

I rose from the bed, my mind churning with theories and possibilities. The pieces of the puzzle were slowly coming together, but the image they formed was still unclear. Who was in that Mercedes? Was it merely a coincidence, or was it the key to unraveling the mystery of Alicia's murder?

As I dressed, my thoughts were interrupted by a sharp knock on the door. I paused, buttoning up my shirt, a sense of anticipation tingling in my nerves. Approaching the door, I wondered who could be seeking me out so early in the morning.

I opened the door to find a man standing in the hallway. He was dressed impeccably in a three-piece suit and tie, his appearance exuding an air of authority and purpose. He was not someone I recognized, yet there was something familiar about his poised demeanor.

"Luigi Ferro, I presume?" he said, his voice calm and measured. "I apologize for the early intrusion, but I believe it is in our mutual interest to have a conversation."

I studied him for a moment, taking in the sharp lines of his suit, the meticulous way his hair was combed back, and the unyielding gaze that met mine. The man's appearance at the school, his formal attire, and the urgency of his visit suggested that he was more than just a casual observer in the unfolding drama. A silent question hanging in the air between us. Who was he, and how did he fit into the complex tapestry of Alicia's murder?

"My name is Valentin Schüss, the Hodler family solicitor," he continued. "May I enter?"

"Of course," I replied, stepping aside to let him in. "What can I do for you?"

I indicated a free chair for him, but he remained standing,

The man cleared his throat, preparing to speak. I braced myself, knowing that whatever he was about to reveal could alter the course of my investigation. In a case shrouded in mystery and deception, every new encounter, every piece of information, brought me one step closer to the truth. And I was determined to uncover it, no matter where it led.

"I understand you are investigating the unfortunate incident involving the late Miss Hodler," Schüss began, his tone polite but firm. "While your efforts are undoubtedly well-intentioned, I must insist that you cease your investigation immediately."

I leaned against the modest desk in my guest room, weighing my response. "Herr Schüss, the school has hired me to uncover the truth behind Alicia Hodler's death. It's about more than just a reputation; it's about justice."

Schüss's lips thinned slightly, a brief flicker of irritation crossing his otherwise composed features.

"The Hodler family has already been through enough, Mr. Ferro. Alicia has been laid to rest in Geneva, and they wish to move on without further disturbance. The family does not share your concern for the school's reputation."

I could sense the unyielding resolve behind his words. This was a man used to having his demands met, unaccustomed to opposition.

"I understand the family's grief," I replied, "but there are still unanswered questions. Someone is responsible for Alicia's death, and the family deserves to know the truth."

Schüss's gaze was unwavering. "The Hodler family has no interest in your investigation, Mr. Ferro. They wish to grieve in peace, away from the prying eyes of the media and private detectives. Your pursuit of this matter is unwelcome."

I couldn't help but feel a surge of frustration. The Hodler family's lack of interest in the investigation was perplexing. Was it simply a desire to avoid scandal, or was there something more they were hiding?

"Herr Schüss, with all due respect, I am not here to cause the Hodler family any further pain," I said, trying to convey my sincerity. "But if there's even a chance that Alicia's death wasn't just a tragic accident, don't you think it's worth investigating? For her sake, if not for the family's?"

Schüss buttoned one button in his impeccable suit jacket, his posture rigid.

"The Hodler family's position is clear, Mr. Ferro. They want nothing to do with this investigation. They have entrusted the management of Hodler Bank and their private affairs to me, and I am here to ensure that their wishes are respected. I strongly advise you to heed this request."

I realized then that there would be no swaying him. Valentin Schüss was a wall, immovable and impassive. His loyalty to the Hodler family was absolute, and he viewed my investigation as nothing more than an unwanted complication.

His final words hung in the air as he left the room, a clear warning. "Leave the Hodler family and their business alone, Mr. Ferro. Consider this matter closed."

I stood alone in the room, the weight of the solicitor's words pressing down on me. The easy thing would be to walk away, to leave the Hodlers to their grief and secrets. But Alicia's haunting image lingered in my mind, a silent plea for the truth.

I knew then that I couldn't let it go. The mystery of Alicia Hodler's death was more than a job; it was a quest for truth in a world where it seemed increasingly elusive. And I was determined to uncover it, no matter the opposition.

*

As I stepped out of the boarding school and into the sunlight, its golden warmth did little to dispel the chill that clung to me. I knew I had to dig deeper and follow the breadcrumbs that Alicia's life had left behind. My gut told me her family's involvement in luxury goods and international banking held the answers I sought.

With Ravenna's history guiding my steps, I dove headfirst into my own investigation. I strolled through the elegant streets of Ravenna, lined with luxury boutiques; my mission was clear yet discreet. I was here to gather information about the brands under the Hodler family's control – a venture into the world of high-end watches, exquisite jewelry, and silk scarves that spoke of wealth and taste. The Hodler family's business dealings, I suspected, might hold clues to the turmoil behind Alicia's tragic demise.

The air was rich with the scent of polished leather and new fabric as I entered the first of many shops, a boutique renowned for its collection of luxury watches. The proprietor, a well-dressed gentleman with a keen eye for detail, greeted me with a mixture of curiosity and caution.

"I'm interested in the Hodler collection," I said, feigning casual interest.

"Ah, the Hodler watches," he began, with a hint of admiration in his tone. "Truly exquisite craftsmanship, but there have been some hiccups lately. Delays in deliveries and errors in orders have left more than a few clients dissatisfied. It's quite unlike their usual standards." He paused, then with a glint in his eye, continued, "Perhaps you'd be interested in exploring our selection of Swiss-made luxury watches? The Patek Philippe is renowned for its impeccable quality and precision."

I nodded, pretending to examine a watch while absorbing his words. It was a small piece of information, yet it hinted at something larger – a crack in the facade of the Hodler empire.

My next stop was a jewelry store, its display windows a dazzling array of diamonds and precious stones. The store owner, an elegant woman in her fifties, was more forthcoming.

"The Hodler jewelry? Beautiful pieces, but it's been difficult to get them lately," she confided after some small talk. "There are whispers, you know, about the family's finances. Some say they're on the brink of bankruptcy."

Bankruptcy. The word hung in the air, heavy with implications. Could the Hodler family's financial troubles be a motive for something more sinister? Was

Alicia's death somehow entangled in a web of financial desperation?

I continued my walk, each visit adding another layer to the picture. At a boutique specializing in silk scarves, the owner, a middle-aged man with a flair for fashion, echoed similar sentiments.

"The Hodler scarves are always in demand," he said, adjusting a display. "But recently, getting them has been a headache. Orders are delayed, and sometimes, the wrong items are sent. It's not good for business, you know."

As I left the shop, the puzzle pieces were slowly forming a coherent image. The Hodler family, known for their wealth and influence, was apparently grappling with financial troubles. Late deliveries and incorrect orders – were signs of a business in distress.

Walking the streets of Ravenna, the city's opulence stood in stark contrast to the hidden struggles of the Hodler empire. The luxury goods that once symbolized their power and status were now whispers of their fading glory.

Could the financial instability of the Hodler family be a key factor in unraveling the mystery of Alicia's death? Could the pressures of maintaining their empire have led to desperate measures?

I pondered these questions as I walked, the city's splendor a mere backdrop to the unfolding drama. The Hodler family, once a symbol of success and luxury, was perhaps a house of cards, teetering on the edge of collapse. And somewhere in this intricate web of high-stakes finance and family secrets lay the truth about what happened to Alicia Hodler.

The Hodler's Bank branch in Ravenna stood like a fortress, its ancient facade a testament to the power and wealth it guarded within. As I pushed open the heavy oak doors, the scent of old money, leather, and hushed secrets filled my nostrils. A chill ran down my spine as if the ghosts of past transactions still lingered in the air.

"Signore," greeted the impeccably dressed bank manager, his eyes flicking over my suit with barely disguised disdain. "What can the Hodler Bank do for you?"

"I'm investigating the murder of Alicia Hodler," I replied, my voice steady and measured. "I believe her family's business dealings may shed light on the motive."

"Surely you understand that our clients' affairs are strictly confidential," he said, a hint of steel beneath his velvet words.

"Of course," I replied smoothly, "but perhaps you could introduce me to some associates who might be more forthcoming." My gaze locked onto his, daring him to refuse me.

"Very well," he acquiesced, leading me through a maze of polished marble and gilded chandeliers. We passed under the watchful gaze of stern-faced portraits, each one silently guarding the secrets they held.

"Here we are," he announced, stopping before a door that seemed no different from the others. He knocked briskly and ushered me inside.

"Luigi Ferro, meet Signor De Luca, a longtime friend of the Hodler family," the bank manager said, stepping aside to reveal a portly man with a thinning hairline and a mustache that bristled with importance. "He can answer your questions."

"Signor De Luca," I began, my tone polite but firm. "As you may know, I am investigating the tragic death of Alicia Hodler. I need to understand her family's business relationships, any potential enemies or rivals."

De Luca eyed me cautiously, his fingers drumming an anxious rhythm on the armrest of his plush leather chair. "The Hodlers have numerous business dealings," he said slowly, weighing each word like a gold coin. "But I cannot think of anyone who would wish them harm."

"Perhaps you could provide a list of their associates?" I pressed. "Names, contact information, anything that might help me piece together the puzzle."

"Signor Ferro, I must respect the privacy of the business," De Luca replied, his voice strained. "I can only tell you they were involved in luxury goods and international banking. Beyond that, my lips are sealed."

I could sense the invisible walls closing in around me, the tantalizing truth just out of reach. Frustration gnawed at my insides, but I refused to show weakness before these men.

"Very well," I said, forcing a smile as I rose to my feet. "Grazie for your time, Signor De Luca."

As I left the bank, a soft breeze carried the sweet scent of jasmine through the narrow streets of Ravenna. The sun cast a golden glow on the ancient city, casting shadows that whispered secrets to those who listened. But the beauty of Ravenna only served to sharpen my senses, and I was determined to unravel the complex web that had entangled Alicia Hodler's life and death.

Slowly, the pieces of the puzzle began to connect. Whispers of financial struggles, hidden debts, and desperate measures floated in the air like stale perfume. A sense of urgency gripped me, urging me forward in my pursuit.

And so, with determination and cunning as my allies, I vowed to unravel the tangled web that had ensnared Alicia Hodler, no matter what dangers lay ahead. The truth awaited in the depths of Ravenna's shadows, and I would not rest until it was mine.

When I returned to the boarding school, I found Miriam Petrilla, the art teacher, waiting outside my room. Her appearance was like a brushstroke on a blank canvas, transforming the mundane corridor into something intriguing.

Miriam was a striking figure, a brunette with hair cascading in loose waves that framed her face, a face that held an intelligent, inquisitive look. She was in her 30s, but there was a timeless quality about her, something that defied easy categorization. Her slim, attractive figure was accentuated by her choice of clothing – simple yet stylish, with an artistic flair that made her stand out.

She moved with an almost hypnotic grace, each step measured and deliberate. There was an air of confidence about her, a quiet assurance that she carried effortlessly.

As she approached, I couldn't help but be drawn to her, her presence filling the room with an undeniable allure.

"Signor Ferro," she said, her voice smooth and melodic, "I heard you've been working on town today, gathering clues for Alicia's case." Her eyes locked onto mine, a depth of emotion swirling within them, reflecting a mixture of curiosity and something akin to a challenge.

"News travels fast in a small city," I replied with a smile, hearing the rumble of my empty stomach. "Would you like to join me for dinner, Signora?"

"Can we not dispense with the formalities, Luigi?" she asked softly, her voice full of longing as she stepped up close to me. "It's just you and me now, and I know just the place for a good bite."

"Very well, Miriam," I replied, my throat dry as she walked next to me, arm-in-arm, each step a graceful dance of temptation.

The night air was heavy with desire, thick like honey, as I followed Miriam Petrilla through the labyrinthine streets of Ravenna. Her lithe silhouette shimmered beneath the moonlight, a mirage that beckoned me toward the precipice of temptation.

"Where are you leading me, Cara?" I asked, my voice barely audible above the susurration of the wind.

"Somewhere we can be alone," she replied, a coy smile playing across her lips. "Do not worry, mio detective, I know the way."

We meandered through the shadowy alleyways, our footsteps echoing against the ancient walls. I couldn't help but marvel at the juxtaposition between the ageless beauty of the city and the enigmatic woman beside me. Both were steeped in history, their secrets buried deep within the foundations of time immemorial.

As we navigated the dimly lit passages, I reached for Miriam's hand, feeling the warmth of her skin against mine. It was both an anchor to reality and a tether to the seductive world she had drawn me into. A part of me knew that I was teetering on the edge of reason, that I should have been focusing on the case before me, but her bewitching allure was too strong to resist.

"Miriam," I breathed, our fingers intertwined as we continued our journey. "What is it about you that has captured me so completely?"

"Perhaps it is our shared love of mystery," she mused, her eyes twinkling with mischief. "Or perhaps it is something more primal – the captivation art of two souls destined to collide."

"Destiny is a fickle mistress," I whispered, my heart pounding like a relentless drumbeat. "But I cannot deny the attraction that binds us together."

Our path took us past the imposing façade of the Hodler's Bank branch, its darkened windows a stark reminder of the treacherous waters I found myself wading through. With each step, I felt the familiar weight of responsibility settle upon my shoulders, as if daring me to unravel the tangled threads of this deadly game.

"Here we are," Miriam announced, stopping before a nondescript door hidden within the shadows. "My home."

"I won't tell a soul," I vowed, stepping across the threshold and into her world.

As the door closed behind us, sealing us away from Ravenna's prying eyes, I knew that our dalliance would have far-reaching consequences. The seeds of seduction had been sown, and there was no turning back.

"Why did you seek me tonight?" I asked.

"Perhaps I wanted to see if there was more to this hardened detective than meets the eye," she whispered, her breath warm against my cheek as she leaned in close. "Or perhaps I am simply drawn to danger."

"Playing with fire, are we?" I queried, my heart thundering in my chest as her fingers traced delicate patterns across my collarbone. "You might get burned."

"Perhaps that is what I desire," she murmured before her lips found mine, igniting a passion that threatened to consume us both.

As we lost ourselves in the embrace of love and lust, the lines between reality and fantasy began to blur. For one fleeting moment, the case and its tangled web faded from my thoughts, replaced by the intoxicating allure of Miriam Petrilla.

But as our bodies entwined and our whispers turned to sighs, the weight of unanswered questions lingered at the edges of my consciousness like a persistent shadow. The stakes were higher than ever, and I knew that the road ahead would be fraught with danger and uncertainty.

"Ravenna," I thought as I stared into Miriam's dark eyes, my senses aflame with desire and trepidation.

"Your mysteries are as deep and inscrutable as the night."

5

The morning sun pierced through the curtains, casting dappled light across the sumptuous sheets that had entwined Miriam and me just hours before. My eyelids fluttered open, and for a moment, I basked in the residue of satisfaction, the scent of Miriam lingering like a promise on my skin. The intoxicating scent of her perfume still lingered in the air, a siren's call beckoning me to abandon reason and succumb to the depths of desire.

"Good morning, Luigi," Miriam whispered, her voice wove into my consciousness. She slipped into a lush silk robe, the fabric clinging lovingly to her every curve. "Did you sleep well?"

"Like a man bewitched," I admitted, watching as she moved with feline grace to the window. She opened the curtains, and the streets of Ravenna stretched out below us, a labyrinth of secrets waiting to be unraveled.

"Time waits for no one, particularly not a private investigator on the trail of a killer," she mused, glancing back at me with a knowing smile. She returned to the bedroom with a steaming hot espresso.

"Indeed," I agreed. I rose, muscles protesting the indulgence, and began to dress. My movements were methodical, an attempt to silence the cacophony of thoughts that threatened to overwhelm the quiet haven we'd created.

As I buttoned my shirt, the taste of espresso lingered

on my tongue, a bitter reminder that reality awaited beyond these walls. I reached for my watch on the dresser next to the untidy bed. A glint of color caught my eye in a half-open drawer.

It was a scarf draped casually amidst the mundane. But this was no ordinary accessory; it was a Hodler Silk, a rare piece that spoke of wealth and whispers in darkened corners. My fingers grazed the fabric, admiring the intricate patterns woven with threads that could unravel far more than just a tapestry.

"Curious about the scarf?" Miriam's voice was a silk thread weaving through the air, pulling at the corners of my attention.

"Seems like a rare find," I responded, watching her silhouette as she moved with feline grace. I pulled out the Hodler Silk from the drawer, its colors vibrant against the muted palette of her lingerie beneath.

"Ah, it was a lucky acquisition," she said, the words floating over her shoulder with practiced nonchalance. "A friend has access to the warehouse where they're stored. Allowed me to purchase it for a trifle."

I leaned against the doorframe, arms crossed. Her explanation danced on a knife-edge between plausibility and deceit. A warehouse? Access to luxury goods wasn't common currency, even in the artful duplicity of Ravenna's social circles.

"Must be quite the friend," I mused, the gears of suspicion grinding in my mind. "Connections like that don't come cheap."

She turned then, her gaze locking onto mine, a smile playing upon her lips that didn't quite reach her eyes. "In this city, Luigi, it's not what you know," she paused, stepping closer, her scent enveloping me, "but who you know."

My pulse quickened, though whether from the proximity of her body or the intrigue of her words, I couldn't say. I felt the fabric of the case fray and intertwine with threads of personal entanglement. My instincts honed from years on the streets whispered warnings as softly as the brush of her fingertips against my chest.

"Indeed," I replied, my voice steady despite the tumultuous thoughts storming within. "And sometimes, it's knowing when to look beneath the surface."

"Always the detective," she teased, her laughter a melody that might have once charmed birds from trees.

"Someone has to be," I retorted, stepping back, reclaiming distance as my ally. The room seemed to shrink, pressing down upon us with the weight of unspoken truths.

With a final glance at the Hodler Silk, I strapped on my watch, the tick of its hands a reminder of the world beyond these walls, of the mystery that lay waiting, insistent and unyielding.

I stood at the threshold of Miriam's townhouse, the dawn morning filtering through the door's frosted glass, casting a matrix of shadows across my exit. I pulled Miriam close, and our lips met in a passionate goodbye.

"Be careful, Luigi." There was a lilt in her tone, playful yet edged with something darker. "Some mysteries bite back."

"Caution is a companion of mine," I assured her before turning on my heel and stepping outside. I started down the narrow street, a piazza at the end gleaming like a beacon of escape. But the serenity of the moment shattered as abruptly as the silence.

A deafening gunshot shattered the quiet, a piercing strike like a venomous viper lashing out. My senses, sharpened from years of living on the edge, took over, and I instinctively dove to the side, feeling the cold metal of a car against my back as I rolled into cover. The sharp smell of hot asphalt filled my nostrils, mixing with the surge of adrenaline coursing through my veins.

"Merda!" The curse slipped from my lips as I surveyed my surroundings. My hand went to my sidearm, fingers closing around the cold metal that promised survival. Nothing seemed amiss, nothing save for the ringing in my ears and the pulsing of my heart—a relentless drumbeat signaling danger.

"Luigi!" Her voice was a siren's call, laced with concern or deceit—I couldn't discern which. "Are you alright?"

"Stay inside!" My command cut through the chaos, my focus narrowing as I pieced together the puzzle before me. The shot had been a warning, a punctuation mark in the conversation of crime and punishment. And I, Luigi Ferro, read between the lines all too well.

I crouched, making my way along the line of parked cars, every sense strained to its limit. The acrid smell of gunfire hung in the air, a stark reminder of the danger that lurked in the shadows.

I crept along the line of parked vehicles, my

senses heightened to every sound, every movement. The metallic taste of fear was in my mouth, and my heart pounded against my ribcage like a caged animal desperate for escape. The street, friendly and sunny just seconds ago, now felt like a labyrinth of dark terror.

With each cautious step, I moved closer to a small Fiat, its windows a potential vantage point. The cars felt like both my shield and my trap, their cold, hard surfaces a meager protection against the unseen assailant.

The street was eerily silent now, the shots having ceased as suddenly as they had begun. I could feel the sweat trickling down my spine, the adrenaline coursing through my veins like fire. I had to know who was behind this attack, who had turned the quiet streets of Ravenna into a battlefield.

Reaching the Fiat, I slowly raised my head, peering through its windows. My eyes scanned the street, searching for any sign of the shooter. The morning sun cast long, ominous shadows, turning every nook and cranny into a potential hiding place for my attacker.

But there was nothing. No movement, no hint of the person who had turned a gun on me. It was as if the shooter had vanished into thin air, leaving behind only the echo of their violence.

I lay there for what felt like an eternity, my body tense, ready to spring into action at the slightest provocation. The silence was oppressive, weighing down on me with the heaviness of unanswered questions. Who had targeted me? Was it related to Alicia's case, a warning to back off? Or was it something more personal, a vendetta against me?

Someone didn't want me digging further in this case.

Finally, I made my decision. I couldn't stay here forever, a sitting duck waiting for the shooter to return. Gathering my courage, I stood up, my eyes constantly moving, searching for any sign of danger.

The street was still empty, the air now filled with the promise of a new day, but all I sensed was foreboding. I moved quickly, keeping to the shadows, my every instinct on high alert. The need to find safety, to escape the open vulnerability of the street, propelled me forward.

As I put distance between myself and the scene of the shooting, I couldn't shake the feeling of being watched. The incident had left its mark, a chilling reminder of the risks that came with delving into the dark underbelly of a seemingly peaceful city.

My mind raced with thoughts of the Hodler family's tangled web, the mysterious Valentin Schüss, and the ever-elusive mastermind whose machinations threatened to bring ruin upon us all.

*

Back in the relative safety of my guest room at the boarding school, the adrenaline of the morning's events slowly ebbed away, replaced by a profound weariness. I sat on the edge of the bed, my mind replaying the harrowing moments on the streets of

Ravenna. The sharp crack of gunshots still echoed in my ears, a grim soundtrack to my racing thoughts.

Who could be behind the shooting? The question circled in my head like a persistent hawk. Was it connected to the Hodler case, a warning to back off? Or something else entirely, a thread I hadn't yet pulled at in this complex tapestry of intrigue and danger?

I rubbed my face wearily, feeling the grit of the rigors on my skin. The room, with its muted colors and soft lighting, was a stark contrast to the streets where death had whispered past me. Here, in this quiet space, the reality of my situation settled heavily upon me. I was a lone player in a game with unseen opponents, with perilously high stakes.

As the tension drained from my body, I lay back on the bed, staring up at the ceiling. The silence of the room enveloped me, a temporary respite from the chaos outside. But even in this moment of peace, I knew the danger was far from over. Someone wanted me gone, silenced, before I could unravel the truth. And I, Luigi Ferro, was not about to let that happen. The mystery of Alicia Hodler's death was more than a job now; it was a personal quest for truth in a world that seemed increasingly shrouded in shadows.

And what about the seductive art teacher?

"Who are you protecting, Miriam?" The question lingered in the air, unanswered, as I examined the cracks in the white-painted ceiling.

"Or is it—what are you hiding?" The thought hung heavy as I brooded on the events of the past days.

A pang of realization struck me then, sharp as the

scent of lemons in summer. Miriam and the murder case — they were interwoven, each a reflection of the other. And I, caught between their threads, felt the prickling sense of impending danger. Had our night of passion been a veil that shrouded a more sinister motive?

My heart drummed a rhythm that matched the cobbled streets beneath me, each beat a question mark, each thrum a doubt. The Hodler Silk scarf — that rare, coveted item — had seemed out of place amidst her modest belongings. A red flag in a sea of white.

And only one person but me knew where I had spent the night. I sat up in bed, ready to continue my investigation.

I knocked on the door with the sign stating its use– Art Studio. As I opened the door to Miriam's art class, a kaleidoscope of colors and shapes greeted me, each student absorbed in their creation. Canvases dotted around the room showcased talent in its raw, unrefined form. Miriam, the epitome of an artist, moved among her students with an almost hypnotic grace. Her comments were a blend of direction and praise, each word encouraging, shaping, and guiding. She was more than a teacher; she was an artist weaving magic into the young minds. Her presence was captivating, a mixture of professionalism and allure. Watching her, it was clear why she was respected and adored in equal measure.

"Signora Petrilla," I called out, my voice slicing through the silence of the studio.

She froze and turned towards me with a smile. A

scent of jasmine trailed behind her like a whispered secret as she approached me. Her eyes held mine with an enigmatic blend of innocence and allure that was as intoxicating as it was treacherous.

"Luigi." Her tone was a caress, a velvet touch against the rough edges of my doubts.

"This morning's gunshot wasn't fired by Cupid's arrow," I said, my words heavy with implication. "And now, amidst this tapestry of deception, even the silken threads seem suspect."

"Whatever do you mean?" She feigned confusion, but a tremor in her gaze betrayed her.

"Your Hodler Silk scarf," I pointed out, sharp as a stiletto. "A rare item, not easily obtained. And yet, it lies casually in your drawer as though it were a mere trinket."

Miriam's lips parted slightly, a breath caught between confession and concealment.

"It was a gift. I told you," she murmured, her voice a serpentine hiss of silk sliding over skin. "From a friend who works at the warehouse."

"Ah, a friend." The word hung between us, laden with unspoken questions. "In my line of work, friends often turn out to be fiends in disguise."

"Is that what you think of me, Luigi?" Her words were slow, deliberate, the dance of the predator circling its prey.

"Sometimes, Miriam, I don't know what to think." My heart was a reluctant drummer, keeping time with caution rather than rhythm.

"Let me ease your mind then." Her fingers grazed my arm, leaving a trail of doubt melting into desire.

"Tell me about this friend," I insisted, my resolve firm, though the temptation of her touch threatened to unravel it.

She cast a glance over her shoulder, noticing that the class was not paying attention to us.

"Romero," she confessed, her voice dropping to a hushed whisper as if the walls themselves were eavesdropping. "He's... complicated, but he has access to things, people."

"Complicated," I echoed, tasting the word on my lips. It was a flavor I knew all too well, a blend of hidden agendas and half-truths. "Is Romero also the kind of friend who would pull a trigger?"

"Luigi, you can't think—"

"Miriam, when it comes to murder, I must consider every possibility," I cut her off, my eyes searching hers for the flicker of guilt or innocence.

"Then consider this," she said, her voice laced with seductive certainty. "I want to help you find the truth."

"Even if the truth implicates you?" The question was a gambit cast upon the waters of her conscience.

"Especially then." Her affirmation was a beacon, illuminating the murky depths of her intentions or perhaps merely another siren call luring me toward treacherous shores.

"Very well," I conceded, watching as the layers of our conversation peeled away, each revelation a strip of cloth removed from the body of the case. "Start by telling me everything you know about Romero, and we'll navigate these dangerous currents together."

"Everything?" A coy smile danced on her lips, promising tales of intrigue and whispers of scandal.

"Every last detail," I affirmed, my voice as resolute as the ancient marble beneath our feet.

"After school, Luigi," she breathed. "Visit me tonight, my lover..."

"Yesterday's enemies can be today's lovers, but tomorrow..." I let the words trail off, the implication hanging between us like the fragrance of her perfume in the air.

"Tomorrow is a mystery yet unwritten," she finished for me, the corner of her lips curving with a knowing smile.

As I stood there, face-to-face with a woman whose secrets were as numerous as the stars above, I knew that weaving through the labyrinth of lies and temptations was the only way to grasp the gossamer strands of truth. And I, Luigi Ferro, would follow them wherever they led, no matter how perilous the path.

I slowly walked back towards my guest room. The dim corridor was partly lit by the afternoon sun shining through the open windows to the inner courtyard. The conversation with Miriam had left me with a heightened sense of awareness. Who was she really, and how was she involved with Romero—the victim's alleged boyfriend?

"Luigi," came a sultry voice, slicing through the stillness like a blade through silk. Amber emerged from the shadows, her presence an intoxicating blend of danger and desire. She leaned against the weathered wall, her white shirt clinging to her curves like morning dew on a ripe peach and the skirt so short I imagined a glimpse of her panties. Her eyes held the promise of secrets untold.

"Miss Boyd-Cohen," I acknowledged, my tone guarded despite the pulse that quickened at her proximity. "To what do I owe the unexpected pleasure?"

"Maybe I just wanted to see you, detective." Her lips curved into a suggestive smile, a potent weapon she wielded with effortless grace. "Or maybe I have something you want."

I eyed her warily, aware of the game she played — a dance of seduction and manipulation where every step could lead to a fall.

"Information doesn't come without a price," I said, my voice low and steady.

"Everything has its price, Luigi." Her hand reached out, fingertips brushing against the lapel of my jacket, a whisper of contact that threatened to unravel my resolve. "But for you, I might be willing to bend the rules–you can have me for free…"

"Cut to the chase, Amber," I urged, stepping back to maintain distance from the siren before me. Her touch was electric, but I needed answers more than I needed another entanglement.

"Romero," she said, her voice dropping to a conspiratorial hush. "He's been seen at a truck distribution center outside the city limits. He does odd jobs there, off the books."

"Romero?" I echoed, my mind racing with the

implications. Romero was the elusive thread in this tapestry of deceit, one that could lead me straight to the heart of the case.

"Yes," she confirmed, pushing herself off the wall and moving closer. "I can take you there, if you're interested. But who knows what we might find along the way?"

The air between us crackled with tension, thick with unspoken desires and dangerous liaisons. I considered her offer, weighing the risks against the burning need for truth that consumed me.

"Just let me know the address," I said with what I thought was a fatherly tone.

"I don't know it," she quipped, minimizing the distance between us. "But I know how to get there."

She pushed her body against mine. "I have no more classes today. Just let me get changed…"

I thought about her offer, her persistence, and her childish seduction.

"Fine," I conceded, the word tasting of both surrender and challenge. "Lead the way."

"Good choice, detective," she purred, satisfaction evident in her voice as she turned to glide down the alley, her hips swaying with confidence.

I followed, my footsteps echoing on the cobblestones, my thoughts a maelstrom of suspicion and anticipation. Amber's revelation was a precarious gift that could either pave the way to resolution or lead me further into temptation's treacherous depths.

We found a taxi, and Amber directed it through the labyrinthine streets; I kept my guard up, knowing that in this city of ancient walls and whispered secrets, every shadow could conceal a knife, and every caress could be laced with poison.

She sat close to me, her hips, thighs, and shoulder constantly pressing against me. She had changed into denim shorts and a black crop top with long sleeves that exposed her flat tummy.

The cab came to a halt as it rolled into the desolate outskirts of Ravenna. The distribution center loomed like a concrete behemoth, shadows clinging to its walls in the waning light. A shiver crawled up my spine—not from the chill in the air, but from the sense of foreboding that hung over this place like a shroud.

Romero had gone missing again, and all leads pointed here, to the underbelly of the city where even the sun seemed reluctant to shine.

"Stay here," I told Amber and gave the driver a wad of notes to keep him happy.

She protested, as expected, clinging to me with her arms around my neck, desperately trying to allow me to let her follow, but I stood my ground.

I closed the car door and stood there for a moment, allowing the silence to wrap around me like a cloak. This was the kind of place where danger didn't just knock on your door—it kicked it down.

I walked along the vast deserted loading bays. No trucks in sight, no workers, not even a lonely crate. Just the hard tarmac under my feet, the unfriendly concrete buildings, and the setting sun.

"Looking for someone?" The voice sliced through the quiet, rough as gravel.

I turned to see a trio of brutes emerging from the twilight, their silhouettes bulky and menacing. I could taste the tension in the air, thick and bitter as black coffee.

"Romero Salvini," I replied, my words measured and cool despite the rising adrenaline. "Heard he might be around."

"Maybe he is, maybe he ain't," the largest one said, stepping forward. His eyes were dark pools of malice.

"Perhaps you gentlemen could assist me in locating him." My voice was steady; I've learned to play it smooth, like velvet over steel.

"Assist? We ain't no concierges," another sneered, the flicker of a switchblade catching the dying light.

"Then consider it a personal favor," I countered, my hand inching towards the inside of my jacket where my own piece of persuasive argument lay concealed.

"Ha! Listen to this guy," the third thug chuckled before lunging at me with the recklessness of a street dog.

Instincts honed by years on the job took over. I sidestepped, grabbing his arm and twisting until I heard the satisfying pop of dislocation. A grunt of pain was his only dialogue.

"Merda!" the leader cursed, swinging a meaty fist towards my face.

I ducked, feeling the whoosh of air as the punch sailed overhead. Time slowed, each second pregnant with possibilities, each movement a dance with death. I pivoted, delivering a sharp jab to his gut and an uppercut that left him gasping for breath.

"Enough of this," I growled, my tone edged with a threat. "Where's Romero?"

"Go to hell," the one with the knife spat, charging at me, blade glinting with malice.

I sidestepped, catching his wrist and giving it a vicious twist. The knife clattered to the ground, its threat extinguished like a candle snuffed out by a cold breeze. With a swift knee to his midsection, I ensured he'd remember our encounter long after tonight.

The first one was back on his feet and lunged at me, his fists swinging wildly. I dodged, feeling the rush of adrenaline fueling my reflexes. I managed to land a quick jab to his gut, but before I could follow up, the second thug was on me.

I grappled with him, trying to use his own momentum against him, but he was surprisingly strong. The alley echoed with the sounds of our struggle, a cacophony of grunts, and the scuffle of shoes on the pavement. Just as I started gaining the upper hand, a heavy blow struck my back, knocking the wind out of me. It was the leader of the trio, a hulking brute with fists like hammers.

I stumbled forward, gasping for air, trying to regain my footing. The leader moved in, his punches relentless and powerful. Each hit felt like a sledgehammer, and I struggled to stay conscious. My vision blurred, and I could feel my strength waning. This was it, I thought. I'm overpowered.

Just then, a loud clang resonated through the alley, and the leader collapsed in front of me, revealing Amber standing behind him, wielding an iron bar with a fierce look in her eyes. She had struck him with a precision that spoke of a hidden strength beneath her youthful exterior.

"Get away from him!" she yelled at the remaining thugs, who, taken aback by the sudden turn of events, hesitated. Seizing the opportunity, I gathered the last vestiges of my strength and launched myself at them. The element of surprise was on our side now, and within moments, the thugs decided they'd had enough, scampering away into the darkness of the night.

I leaned heavily against the wall, trying to catch my breath, feeling the bruises and pain starting to set in. Amber approached, her eyes filled with concern.

"Are you okay, Luigi?" she asked, her voice a mix of worry and relief.

I tried to straighten up, to show some semblance of composure, but my body betrayed me, and I winced in pain.

"I've been better," I managed to say, forcing a weak smile.

Without a word, Amber slipped her arm around me, supporting me as we made our way back to the waiting taxi. Her touch was gentle yet firm, and I couldn't help but feel a sense of gratitude mixed with a surprising warmth towards her.

As we settled into the taxi, I glanced at Amber, noticing for the first time the fire in her eyes, the determination that had driven her to come to my rescue. She was more than just a sex-crazed student; she was a force to be reckoned with.

The drive back was a blur, my body aching and my

mind reeling from the night's events. But through it all, Amber was there, a steady presence in the chaos. As we neared the boarding school, I realized that this case was changing me, revealing layers and depths in people I had never expected to find. And Amber Boyd-Cohen, the young student who had saved me, was a testament to that.

6

My head pounded like a jackhammer on ancient cobblestones, and my vision swam as I tried to focus on the room. The scent of jasmine infiltrated my nostrils, unfamiliar yet intoxicating. I blinked several times, trying to clear the fog that enveloped me.

"Where am I?" I muttered to myself, wincing at the sound of my own voice.

Soft silk sheets brushed against my naked skin, and I felt the warmth of another body next to mine. Turning my head, I found Amber lying beside me, her golden hair cascading over her shoulders like a silken waterfall. Her eyes fluttered open, immediately locking onto mine with a sultry gaze.

"Buongiorno, Ferro," she purred, a playful smile gracing her lips. "I was hoping you'd wake up soon."

"Amber, what happened?" I asked, trying to sit up but feeling a sharp pain in my side. "Why am I here?"

"Easy, tough guy," she cooed, gently pushing me back down. "You're injured, remember? Let me take care of you."

She reached for a small jar on the bedside table, dipping her fingers into its contents – some kind of ointment, it seemed. Her touch was gentle as she applied the salve to my bruises, her fingers leaving trails of fire in their wake.

"Amber, I need answers," I said, gritting my teeth

and attempting to push past the searing sensation. "Tell me what happened."

"Shh," she whispered, pressing a finger to my lips and leaning in close. "Just relax. You'll get your answers when you're better."

Her breath was warm on my face, her perfume dizzying. It took every ounce of willpower I possessed not to give in to the temptation of her touch. As she continued to treat my wounds, her hands glided over me with the practiced ease of a seductress well-versed in the art of distraction. But I couldn't afford to lose myself in her embrace – not when there was a mystery to be solved.

"Amber," I said, grabbing her wrist gently as she moved to apply more ointment to my shoulder. "I don't have time for games. Tell me what happened."

"Very well," she sighed, capitulating with a hint of disappointment in her eyes. "Do you remember the fight? You were attacked. I found you and brought you here to a small hotel. You're safe now."

"Attacked?" I asked, searching my memory and an image of the distribution center, and the three assailants slowly emerged from the darkness and pain.

"Yes, darling," Amber confirmed, her eyes darkening with concern. "You're lucky I managed to cut in when I did. Who knows what would've happened otherwise?"

"Thank you," I murmured, feeling a strange mix of gratitude and unease. Though I knew Amber had saved me, something about the situation gnawed at me, like the gentle lapping of waves against the shore, slowly eroding my trust in her intentions.

The pain was sharp, an unwelcome guest in my battered body, yet the scene unfolding before me offered a distraction. Amber, young and obviously skilled in the art of nursing, was tending to my injuries with a gentle and precise touch. Her fingers moved over my skin, easing the pain, their touch as soothing as any balm.

She moved with a grace that seemed almost otherworldly, her body glistening with the effort. The air was filled with her scent, an intoxicating blend of lavender and jasmine. Despite the pain, I found myself drawn to her, unable to resist the pull of her youthful allure.

As she leaned in closer, her breath warm against my neck, a shiver ran down my spine. I could feel the softness of her body against mine, the heat of our skin mingling. Her lips traced a line along my jaw, sending a jolt of desire through me.

"You are so strong," she whispered. Her words were like a melody, sweet and charming.

Her hands, no longer just treating my wounds, lingered on my skin, her touch becoming more intimate, less about healing and more about exploration. Each brush of her fingers sent a current of electricity through me, igniting a fire I struggled to control.

She paused, looking up at me with eyes that sparkled with mischief.

"I know just how to make you feel better," she murmured, her voice a seductive promise. She leaned in, her lips grazing my earlobe, her movements deliberate and teasing.

Unable to resist, I responded to her advances. She was intoxicating, her presence a heady mix of innocence and seduction. She pulled away the smooth sheets and straddled me, her body fitting perfectly against mine. The feeling of her, so close and so warm, was overwhelming.

Her breasts grazed against my chest, and I couldn't help but notice the perfect symmetry of them—full and round, taut nipples brushing against my chest.

She began to grind against me slowly, her hips moving in a rhythm that matched the pounding of my heart. I groaned, unable to resist any longer. She was exquisite, intoxicating. I reached up to pull her closer, my fingers tangling in her silken hair.

Her lips found mine, hot and demanding. Our tongues danced together in a sensual waltz as our bodies moved in unison. She tasted like sweet wine and secrets, intoxicating and forbidden. I lost myself in the kiss, giving in to the desire that had been simmering beneath the surface since we first met.

Her blue eyes were dark with desire. Lost in each other, we gave in to the passion, our moans a testament to the intensity of our connection. At that moment, all caution was forgotten, all pain eclipsed by the overwhelming sensation of being with her.

*

Amber Boyd-Cohen proved to be a skilled lover, and as we lay panting side-by-side, I had almost forgotten about the pain, but I couldn't shake the feeling that the truth of Alicia's death was within my grasp – I just couldn't see it yet.

The late morning sun cast its warm, golden glow upon the facade of the school as Amber and I approached, keeping a safe distance as any guilty lovers. The air was heavy with the scent of Mediterranean pines and a faint whisper of jasmine, intoxicating my senses as if to lull me into a false sense of security. But the scene that awaited us shattered any illusions of tranquility.

"Madonna," I muttered under my breath, taking in the chaotic tableau laid out before us. Police cars and ambulances had descended upon the school like vultures eager to feast on the carnage within. Sirens blared, their discordant wails echoing off the ancient walls, drawing forth memories of centuries past when battles were fought, and lives were lost on these very grounds.

"Something terrible has happened," Amber murmured, her voice barely audible above the cacophony. She grabbed my hand tightly, fingers trembling ever so slightly, betraying her carefully composed facade.

"Si," I agreed, my gaze scanning the sea of blue uniforms and white coats swarming around us like ants on a discarded morsel. The tall, slim figure of Madame Merola caught my eye. She was standing at the edge of the chaos, hands on her hips and a scowl etched onto her gray face.

"Ah, Ferro," the headmistress called out as we neared her, her voice authoritative yet caring. "We have looked for you."

Her gaze fell upon the young woman beside me.

"Signorina Boyd-Cohen," she said, her eyes wide and filled with an intoxicating blend of fear and curiosity. "Go to your room."

"Luigi," Amber whispered, tiptoeing, her breath warm against my ear, sending shivers down my spine despite the heat of the day. "Seek me out later..."

I nodded in silence, my focus on the turmoils around us.

"What happened here, Madame?" I asked the headmistress whose iron grip held sway over this institution.

"Signor Muro has been found dead." Her voice was as sharp and precise as the tailored lines of her elegant black suit. "I assume you know of him?"

"Not really," I replied, studying her carefully composed features for any hint of emotion. The headmistress was as inscrutable as ever, a master of deception who concealed her true self behind layers of refined silk and calculated words. "I have yet to interview him. Can you tell me?"

"He was our groundskeeper. Had been with us for about three years, and he has..."

"He came here at the same time as Alicia Hodler then?" I interrupted.

She took a second in silence to think, then nodded before continuing. "...and he has been a real asset. Also helping the students with crafts and gardening."

"Don't you find it strange that two individuals who came here at the same time now are dead?" I probed.

As Madame Merola didn't reply, I continued. "May I see the scene?"

"Of course," she replied, leading me through the crowd to the inner courtyard and to the small workshop built against the far inner wall.

As we entered the workshop, I was struck by the macabre tableau before me: Gerardo Muro's lifeless body slumped over his workbench, crimson seeping into the once-pristine wooden planks under the body. His eyes stared blankly at the ceiling, a silent plea for mercy that had gone unanswered.

"Who found him?" I asked, my gaze lingering on the corpse and the secrets it held.

"Miriam," Madame Merola replied, her voice betraying the faintest hint of concern. "They were… friendly."

"Friendly, how?" I pressed, my instincts honed by years of experience sensing the hidden currents that flowed beneath her words.

"Relationships, Signor Ferro," she sighed, a note of resignation creeping into her tone. "The tangled webs of desire and temptation that so often ensnare the unwary."

"Perhaps," I mused, eyeing the room with renewed interest, each detail revealing itself like layers of fine silk slipping away to expose the raw truth beneath. "But this scene speaks of more than a friendly folly. This is a tale of power, twisted passions, and secrets buried deep within these ancient walls."

"Then it falls to you," Madame Merola said, fixing me with a piercing stare that challenged me to unravel the enigma that had claimed one of her own, "to bring those secrets into the light."

No sooner had the words left Madame Merola's lips than the heavy doors of the office were thrust open, the swirling mist of the outside world creeping in like ghostly fingers seeking purchase on the room's dark secrets. The man who entered was as imposing as the night itself, his worn features and creased suit a testament to a man constantly on the job.

"Commissario Ettora Scarpa," he announced, his voice a low growl that betrayed years of suppressed rage. "What are you doing here, Ferro?" His gaze bore into me like a dagger, each word dripping with contempt.

"Ah, Commissario," I replied, my tone smooth as polished marble, "always a pleasure to see you as well. I'm simply lending my expertise to this little mystery."

"Your 'expertise' is not needed nor wanted," Scarpa hissed, his eyes narrowing to dangerous slits. "I've handled cases of far greater importance than this without interference from private investigators."

"Be that as it may," I said, refusing to rise to his bait, "I have already made some interesting observations." I gestured towards the body of Gerardo Muro, the scent of copper and ink heavy in the air. "This is no simple crime of passion or youthful indiscretion. There are deeper forces at play, hidden beneath layers of deceit and secrecy."

"Va bene," Scarpa acquiesced, his disdain barely concealed behind a mask of grudging cooperation. "Tell me what you've found, but make it quick. Time is of the essence."

I began, telling the story as far as I knew it.

Leaving out irrelevant parts, such as my involvement with Miriam and Amber, but including my search for Romero and the shots fired at me yesterday. I ended with the Hodler family's solicitor and the assault at the distribution center.

"Your theories are as fanciful as they are useless," Scarpa scoffed, though I could see the flicker of uncertainty behind his eyes. "This is a matter for the police, and we will conduct our own investigation and determine the truth in due time."

"By all means, Commissario," I replied, stepping towards the door. "But while you sift through the detritus of lives long past, I will follow a lead that has presented itself, one that may bring us closer to finding the culprit behind all this."

"It's a free country, Ferro," Scarpa shrugged, his voice tinged with an uncharacteristic edge of concern. "The path upon which you tread leads to dangerous places, and the shadows you seek to illuminate may yet consume you."

And with that, I stepped into the courtyard, the seductive allure of secrets yet to be uncovered drawing me deeper into the heart of the Umbri International School and the sinister world that lay hidden just beneath its sun-kissed surface.

My walk brought me through the empty school; all classes had been suspended, and I reached the Art Studio. As I stepped inside, a beguiling scent of paint and turpentine filled the air, weaving a spell of seduction that ensnared my senses. It was here that I found Miriam, her beauty a beacon amidst the gloom. She stood before an easel, slowly stroking the paintbrush over the canvas. Each movement was like a lover's caress.

"Miriam," I said, approaching her slowly, my voice barely audible. "We need to talk."

She turned to face me, her eyes brimming with unshed tears, their emerald depths reflecting the pain she harbored within.

"Luigi," she whispered, her voice trembling with emotion. "Have you heard about Gerardo... it's unbearable."

"Tell me what you know," I urged, guiding her to a secluded corner where our conversation could remain shrouded in secrecy.

"Gerardo and I... we were close," Miriam confessed, her gaze fixed on the flickering shadows that played upon the floor. "And he knew Romero. They were friends long before I met them."

"Did Muro ever mention anything about their relationship?" I asked, my mind racing as I attempted to piece together the fragments of the puzzle that lay before me.

"Only that they shared a bond forged in hardship," she replied, her voice heavy with sorrow. "A bond that somehow tied them to the darkness that now surrounds us all."

"Miriam, I need you to trust me," I said, my eyes locked with hers as I sought to convey the urgency of our situation. "The truth is like your painting, changing its colors to suit the whims of those who wield the brush. But together, we can strip away the layers of deceit and lay bare the heart of this mystery."

"Very well, Luigi," she acquiesced, her determination evident in the set of her jaw and the fire that burned within her eyes. "I will do whatever it takes to bring those responsible for Gerardo's death to justice."

"Then let us begin," I murmured, the weight of our shared resolve settling upon my shoulders like a mantle of steel.

We left the school behind and walked side-by-side without a goal and for no other point than talking in private. A sultry breeze whispered secrets through the narrow streets, carrying with it the heavy scent of jasmine and temptation. The cobblestones beneath our feet echoed the pounding of our hearts, a syncopated rhythm that seemed to beat in unison with the pulse of Ravenna's veiled underbelly.

"Luigi," Miriam murmured, her voice like velvet on my skin, "where do we begin? How can we hope to untangle the twisted webs of deceit that enshroud this sordid affair?"

"Ah, Cara mia," I replied, the ghost of a smile touching my lips. "It is by following the slender threads of desire, temptation, and seduction that we will uncover the truth that lies hidden within the shadows." I glanced at her face, pale and luminous in the moonlight, her eyes pools of liquid darkness that seemed to call out to me, beckoning me to plunge into their depths.

"First, we must retrace the steps of Gerardo Muro and his connection to Romero," I said softly, my thoughts turning inward as I sought to unravel the intricacies of this complex tapestry. "We know that they were both involved in something far more dangerous than simple dalliances with students."

"Romero was also connected to the solicitor," Miriam interjected, her fingers tightening reflexively around my arm. "And the solicitor... he had ties to powerful people in town. People who would not want their secrets exposed."

"Really," I mused, the pieces of the puzzle beginning to coalesce in my mind, forming a tableau as vivid and intricate as the frescoes that adorned the walls of Ravenna's ancient churches.

I stopped. Miriam took a few steps before realizing I was not by her side. I dialed a number on my cell and lifted the device to my ear.

"Commissario," I said. "Can I trust in your discretion and a small favor?"

I explained what I needed, and within a minute, he delivered the information.

"Let's meet at the school in thirty minutes." I ended the call.

"This is a real game of shadows, with willing participants in a dance of seduction and betrayal that has been choreographed by someone cunning and ruthless."

"Who?" Miriam breathed, her eyes wide with apprehension.

"Ah, that, Cara, is the question that burns at the heart of this mystery," I replied, my voice heavy with the gravity of our quest. "But it is a question to which

I am certain the answer lies waiting, concealed within the folds of Ravenna's present and the tangled web of power and desire that blinds people."

As the evening pressed down upon us, the darkness seemed to breathe with the weight of a thousand secrets, a cacophony of whispers that taunted us with their elusive promises of revelation. Yet, even as we navigated the treacherous currents of deception and intrigue that threatened to ensnare us at every turn, I could not help but be acutely aware of the woman who walked beside me, her beauty and courage a beacon of hope amidst the gathering storm.

"Luigi," she said softly, her fingers brushing mine like a stolen caress. "I have faith in you. Together, we will uncover the truth and lay bare the heart of this conspiracy."

"Yes, dear," I replied, the fire of Miriam's belief in me igniting a fierce determination within my own soul. "Together, we shall strip away the veil of secrecy and expose the mastermind behind this sordid affair, no matter how deeply they may be entrenched within the folds of this illustrious tapestry."

For it was at that moment that I knew, beyond the shadow of a doubt, that the answer to this enigma lay hidden within a darkness as ancient and inscrutable as the city itself, a darkness that would yield its secrets only to those who possessed the courage to face it unflinching. And in Miriam's eyes, I saw reflected the fierce light of our shared determination, a flame that burned with a passion as intense and all-consuming as the very heart of Ravenna herself.

7

The scent of rich coffee and the hum of whispers wafted through the air as I stepped into Madame Merola's dimly lit office. She stood behind her mahogany desk, elegant as ever in her tailored suit, a piece that clung to her curves like a secret whispered between lovers. Commissario Ettora Scarpa leaned against the windowsill, his steely eyes cutting through the haze of cigarette smoke.

"Signor Ferro," Madame Merola purred, "we've been waiting for you. What have you uncovered?"

"Madame," I began, savoring the way her name rolled off my lips like silk against skin. "I've untangled this web of deceit, and the truth is more insidious than we could've imagined."

"Cut the theatrics, Ferro," Scarpa interjected, his voice coarse as stale bread. "Who's behind Alicia's murder?"

"Patience, Commissario," I replied, allowing a wry smile to play upon my lips. "Unfortunately for Alicia, she made the grave mistake of falling for Romero Salvini. That devious man had been orchestrating illegal dealings at the Hodler goods distribution center, purposefully misplacing and delaying deliveries to make a profit for his actual employer. Not only did his actions bring shame upon the Hodler brand, but it was enough to make her a target when she found out about it."

"Romero?" Madame Merola's chest heaved with indignation, her breath catching like a cat on velvet. "But why would he involve himself with my student?"

"Desire has a way of making us dance with the devil, Madame," I mused. "But it wasn't Romero who orchestrated this twisted plot. No, the mastermind lies much closer to home."

"Who, then?" Scarpa demanded, his fists clenched like a vice around his unlit cigarette.

"Someone we least suspected," I said, locking eyes with the headmistress. "Someone within these very walls."

"Who?" she breathed, her pupils dilating like a forbidden secret unfurling in the shadows.

"Signor Muro, the groundskeeper," I revealed, the words dripping from my tongue like honey laced with poison. "He was placed here by a competing business to keep an eye on Alicia and report back to them."

"Impossible!" Madame Merola gasped, her hand flying to her throat as if to choke back the truth.

"Believe it or not, Madame," I said, feeling the weight of justice settle upon my shoulders. "I believe young Romero Salvini will sing like a whole gospel choir as you interview him, Commissario. Romero recognized the men in the black Mercedes that sped away from the shooting and disappeared as he got scared. He finally realized what the men he was working for were capable of."

"Damn," Scarpa muttered, crushing his cigarette beneath the heel of his dusty shoe. "I never saw this coming."

"Few ever do, Commissario," I replied, my gaze lingering on the headmistress as she struggled to compose herself. "But that's the nature of desire, temptation, and power. They weave a story more intricate than any Italian tapestry, leaving us entwined in their threads, desperate for release."

A symphony of sirens wailed in the distance, the crescendo of justice drawing near. The sanguine glow of the setting sun draped itself over the school grounds like a temptress's silken negligee, casting shadows that danced and whispered secrets yet untold. As I sat down, my throat ached for the familiar solace of gin and lime.

"Luigi, who was behind all this?" Madame Merola asked, her voice a trembling aria of fear and longing as she clutched her shawl tightly around her slim shoulders.

"Valentin Schüss," I replied, my voice low and velvety, like the caress of an illicit lover. "He's a solicitor involved in a competing business."

"Valentin Schüss?" she repeated, her dark eyes widening like black holes, threatening to swallow up her disbelief. "But how did you...?"

"Sometimes, Madame, one must venture into the labyrinth of desire and deceit, tracing the threads of temptation and power until they unravel the tapestry of truth," I said, the words spilling from my lips like liquid silk.

"Those threads led me to Schüss, who orchestrated Alicia's murder to protect his interests," I continued, the bitter taste of revelation lingering on my tongue. "And now, he will pay for his sins."

"Will it bring her back?" Madame Merola murmured, her gaze lost in the swirling chiaroscuro of the twilight sky.

"Sadly, no," I admitted, my heart heavy with the knowledge of lives forever altered by greed and ambition. "But it will bring closure and justice to those left behind."

"Justice," she echoed, the word slipping from between her rouged lips like a sigh of surrender.

"Indeed, madame," I affirmed, my gaze locked onto hers, the electric charge of truth pulsating between us. "The ultimate aphrodisiac for those who hunger for it."

"Your words are as intoxicating as your presence, Signor Ferro," she breathed, her eyes flickering like the flame of a dying candle. "You have opened my eyes to the shadows that lurk beneath the veneer of respectability."

"Sometimes, Madame," I replied, the soft sibilance of my words weaving a seductive spell, "the most potent secrets are hidden beneath the finest fabric of our lives."

The sun dipped below the horizon, its final rays painting the sky in hues of blood and gold. I stood at the edge of the school courtyard, the scent of freshly watered earth and crushed jasmine blossoms heavy upon the air. Students, teachers, and police officers mingled like dancers at a masquerade ball, their faces painted with a heady blend of relief and disbelief.

"Signor Ferro," murmured Commissario Scarpa, his voice as smooth and dark as aged Amarone, "we have dispatched our men to apprehend Romero Salvini and Valentin Schüss."

"His tentacles reach far and wide, Commissario," I replied, my eyes fixed on the ever-shifting tapestry of shadows that cloaked the ancient stone walls. "I trust you will do your best."

"Indeed," he agreed, his fingers curling around a glass of Barolo like a lover's caress. "And the AlpenGuild Corporation will soon find itself scrutinized by eyes that see beyond the veil of deception."

"La verità prevale sempre," I whispered, my heart swelling with a fierce pride that burned like the fire of a thousand suns.

"Si, si," Scarpa concurred, raising his glass in a silent toast to the triumph of truth over deception.

*

The next morning, I packed my bag and was ready to leave. My job in Ravenna concluded. I had a ticket for the train back this afternoon and was going to meet Alicia's parents after breakfast; they had flown in from Geneva.

There was a shy knock on my door, and as I opened it, I found the cute blonde student Amber Boyd-Cohen outside. Dressed in her school uniform and an enigmatic smile.

"Amber," I greeted her friendly.

"Hi, Luigi," she said, stepping into my room, her voice as sweet and clear as a silver bell. "What will become of Romero?"

"His sins will be weighed against his suffering, dear," I assured her, my gaze lingering on the delicate curve of her bosom, exposed by the careless tilt of her head. "For even in the darkest depths of corruption, there lies a glimmer of redemption."

"Your wisdom is astounding," she smiled, her eyes shining like polished emeralds in the fading light.

"Ah, bella ragazza," I murmured, my thoughts drifting like silk upon a warm summer breeze. "If only wisdom were enough to shield us from the insidious allure of temptation."

"Perhaps it is not wisdom alone that protects us, Luigi," she said, her words as fragile and beautiful as the petals of a rose. "But the strength and courage to face the shadows within our own hearts."

"Indeed," I agreed, smiling, my soul stirred by the depths of her insight. "For it is within those shadows that our true selves lie hidden, waiting for the moment when desire and destiny collide with the force of a tempest-tossed sea."

"Then let us hope that we are strong enough to weather the storm," she whispered, the promise of unspoken secrets dancing within the depths of her eyes.

"Si, cara mia," I replied, my heart aching with the knowledge that even the fiercest love can be torn asunder by the cruel hand of fate. "Per l'amore è il nostro faro nella notte più oscura."

"What?" she replied with raised eyebrows.

"For love is our lighthouse in the darkest night," I mused.

"Ah, you Italians," she quipped. "Love and amore. Always."

"I'm not Italian," I corrected her. "I'm Sammarinese, from San Marino."

"Anyway," she said, stepping up close to me. "Thank you for sorting out this with Alicia. I'll be able to find closure."

She tiptoed and gave me a kiss that I thought I would savor for a long time.

The door flung open at the moment she took a step back, and Miriam rushed inside.

"Luigi! Are you leaving without saying goodbye?" She almost shouted but stopped in her tracks as she saw Amber in front of me.

"Did I interrupt?" Her tone was not apologetic nor questioning; it was insinuating.

"Nothing that can't be interrupted," I replied, regaining my composure. Miriam's arrival had jolted me back to reality, a reminder of the many threads still unraveling in this complex case.

With a cheeky smile, Amber slipped away, leaving a trail of mixed emotions in her wake.

Miriam moved closer, her artist's eyes observing me as if I were a subject in one of her paintings.

"So, where does this leave the investigation?" she inquired, her tone shifting to a more serious note.

"Miriam," I began, my voice steady, "we need to lay out everything we know and see where we stand."

She nodded, her eyes reflecting the gravity of the situation.

As I recounted the events, from the tragic demise of Alicia to the unsettling encounters with the thugs, a pattern emerged, one that was as intricate as it was disturbing. I talked about Romero's fear, the mysterious black Mercedes, and the financial troubles plaguing the

Hodler empire. But one piece of the puzzle remained out of place, a detail gnawed at me.

"Miriam," I said, turning to face her, "something about the shooting doesn't add up. Why was I targeted?"

She hesitated, a flicker of something crossing her face. At that moment, I knew. Taking a step closer, I could feel the tension between us, an electric current in the air.

"Miriam, did you tell anyone I spent that night with you?" My voice was low, a growl that barely concealed the undercurrent of betrayal I felt.

Her eyes dropped a silent admission. "Yes, I... I told Muro," she whispered, her voice barely audible. "I didn't think—"

I cut her off, my emotions boiling over. In two strides, I was in front of her, my hand pressing against the wall beside her head.

"You didn't think? Miriam, that shooting could have been the end of me!" The words came out harsh, a torrent of frustration and disbelief.

She looked up at me, her eyes wide, remorseful.

"I'm sorry, Luigi. I never meant for any harm to come to you. I did not know about his connections…" Her voice was a plea; her usual composure shattered.

We stood there, the air charged with unsaid words and unspent emotions. The distance between us was minimal, yet it felt like a chasm. I could see the turmoil in her eyes, the realization of the consequences of her actions.

Slowly, I stepped back, the anger ebbing away, replaced by a weary resignation.

"This case is closed, Miriam. But it's bigger than either of us realized."

She nodded, her usual grace returning as she composed herself.

"I understand, Luigi. I'll be more cautious."

As we prepared to part ways, there was a pause in time, where everything seemed to stand still. I looked at her, really looked at her, seeing not just the art teacher or the unwitting informant but Miriam in all her complexity.

And then, almost impulsively, we leaned in, our lips meeting in a kiss that was a mix of apology, understanding, and a hint of something more. It was a kiss that spoke of shared experiences, secrets, and dangers navigated together.

We broke apart, the echo of the kiss lingering between us.

"Goodbye, Miriam," I said, my voice soft.

"Goodbye, Luigi," she replied, her voice tinged with a sadness that mirrored my own.

*

The air was thick with grief as I met with the Hodler family amidst the ancient columns, their marble surfaces veined with history. The two parents were impeccably dressed, and tears shimmered like liquid diamonds upon their cheeks.

"Signor Ferro," murmured Alicia's mother, her voice a velvet whisper that caressed the raw edges of my soul. "We are grateful for your tireless pursuit of the truth."

"The truth is a demanding lady, Signora," I replied,

my gaze drawn to the portrait of Alicia that they brought with them, her beauty captured in vibrant strokes of color that seemed to breathe life into the very fabric of the canvas.

"Indeed, it is," she said, her eyes reflecting the pain that lay hidden beneath her stoic facade. "Yet even in the face of tragedy, we must find the strength to persevere."

"Si, Signora," I agreed, my thoughts turning to the tangled web of deceit and betrayal that had woven itself around the fragile threads of Alicia's life, ensnaring her within its deadly embrace. "But let us not forget that it is in our darkest hour that the light of truth shines brightest."

"Your words offer solace, Signor," whispered Alicia's father, his once-powerful frame now bowed beneath the weight of anguish and regret. "For though our daughter has been taken from us, her memory shall forever burn like a beacon within our hearts."

"Ah, Signor Hodler," I murmured, my hand resting upon his shoulder in a gesture of comfort and understanding. "There is no greater tribute to a life well-lived than the love and admiration of those left behind."

"Yet there remains so much unsaid," he admitted, his voice choked with emotion as his gaze lingered upon the image of his beloved child. "So many questions that will forever haunt us. But I expect our business in Italy to pick up." He forced a smile.

"I sincerely hope so, Signor," I said, my heart heavy with the knowledge that some answers would remain shrouded in the shadows of the past. "It is in our quest for understanding that we ultimately find peace and acceptance."

"True, Signor Ferro," Alicia's mother agreed, her eyes meeting mine with a depth of gratitude that defied words. "For it is only through the bitter trials of adversity that we learn to cherish the moments of joy and happiness that fate has granted us."

"Si, Signora," I whispered, my thoughts drifting like smoke upon the winds of time, carrying with them the bittersweet memories of a love lost and a promise unfulfilled. "May we all find solace in the knowledge that, though the tempests of life may rage around us, the flame of hope shall never be extinguished."

"Forever in our hearts," she murmured, her words a tender benediction that echoed the eternal bond of family and the resilience of the human spirit.

Mr. Hodler pressed a folded check into the palm of my hand, ensuring my income for months to come.

"Forever," I repeated, my soul aching with the beauty and fragility of life's fleeting embrace. For even as the shadows of sorrow threatened to engulf us, a sliver of light pierced the darkness, illuminating the path toward healing and redemption.

*

Through the haze of a dying afternoon, I stood on the steps of Umbri International School, my gaze sweeping over the throng of reporters, cameramen, and curious onlookers that had descended upon the palazzo like a swarm of ravenous vultures. The scent of warm streets and sweaty people hung heavy in the air, mingling with the acrid stench of burning tobacco as the whispers of scandalous intrigue danced upon the breeze.

"Luigi! Luigi Ferro!" a familiar voice called out to me, cutting through the cacophony of murmurs and camera shutters. Turning towards the source, I found myself face to face with Caterina, her eyes sparkling with mischief behind the lens of an SMTV news camera.

"Ah, Caterina," I sighed, my heart quickening beneath the weight of her sultry gaze. "I should have known they'd send you to cover this sordid little denouement."

"Indeed," she purred, her lips curling into a tantalizing smile that sent shivers down my spine. "After all, a Sammarinese hero solves an international murder case filled with mystery and desire?"

"Mr. Ferro," she continued, her voice professional yet tinged with a hint of challenge, "you've solved a case that seemed to elude the Italian police. How did a Sammarinese private investigator manage that?"

The camera's unblinking eye was fixed on me, capturing every nuance, every flicker of emotion. I adjusted in my seat, feeling the weight of her question.

"Well," I started, choosing my words carefully, "sometimes being an outsider helps. You see things from a different perspective."

I leaned forward slightly, aware of the camera's gaze. "In San Marino, we have a saying, 'small but mighty.' It's not about the size of the place you come from but the depth of your determination. My approach to this case was methodical and patient. It wasn't about outdoing the police but about finding the truth in the details they might have overlooked."

Caterina nodded, her expression softening slightly. "So, it's your attention to detail and persistence that made the difference?"

"Exactly," I replied, feeling a sense of pride. "Every case has its own rhythm, its own unique set of clues. It's about listening to that rhythm and understanding the story it's trying to tell. That's what I did."

As the interview wrapped up, and before other media had the chance to approach me, I asked if she could give me a lift home.

The sun dipped low in the sky as I returned to San Marino, the warm hues of orange and pink painting the horizon like a master's brushstroke. A familiar sense of relief washed over me as Caterina drove the SMTV van through the winding streets. Her dark hair flowed like silk in the wind from the open side window, a symbol of the temptations that I could never quite resist.

"Feels good to be back, doesn't it?" she said, her voice barely audible above the engine's rumble.

"Si, but there's still much to ponder," I replied, my thoughts already drifting to the case I had just closed. The weight of my uncovered secrets pressed down on me, a heavy reminder of the darkness that lurked beneath even the most picturesque facades.

As she pulled up to my small apartment, Caterina kissed me gently on the cheek. "I'll leave you to your thoughts, Ferro. Call me when you're ready for a distraction."

"Thank you, cara mia," I murmured, watching her drive away, thinking of the pleasurable distractions she was capable of. But for now, I needed solitude to process the tangled web of deceit and corruption I had untangled.

The evening stretched before me, quiet and unassuming. It was a welcome contrast to the frenetic energy of the case I'd left behind. I poured myself a gin, the twist of lime a sharp counterpoint to the smooth liquor, and sank into my favorite armchair.

The room around me was dimly lit; the soft glow from the candles in my old brass candlestick cast flickering shadows on the walls. The scent of aged leather and tobacco lingered in the air, a comforting balm against the world's harsh realities outside.

Sipping my drink, I stared into the darkness, allowing my thoughts to drift back to the case. A tangled web of desire and temptation, it had threatened to consume me, pulling me ever deeper into its seductive embrace. But in the end, I emerged victorious, another testament to my steadfast pursuit of truth and justice.

Yet, the victory was bittersweet. The cost of exposing the dark underbelly of power and ambition weighed heavily on my conscience, the lives forever altered by the machinations of others, a constant reminder of the fragility of human existence.

Truth is always bitter, but it is a burden I willingly bear, for without it, we are lost.

As the evening wore on, the shadows lengthening until they consumed the last vestiges of daylight, I found solace in the quiet stillness of my solitary contemplation. For there, amidst the silence, lay the seeds of understanding, the first steps toward healing the wounds wrought by the darker aspects of our nature.

As I closed my eyes, the memories of the case fading like the embers of a dying fire, I knew that when the dawn came, I would be ready to face whatever challenges awaited me, fortified by the knowledge that even in the darkest of times, the light of truth always prevails.

*

I enjoyed an undisturbed, dreamless sleep that didn't end until midday. Waking up at home was comforting, but the thoughts of the case still lingered in my mind and left me craving solace, a refuge from the tempest of brooding that raged within. Where better to find it than at Caffè delle Ombre, my sanctuary amidst the labyrinthine streets of San Marino? Its scent, an intoxicating blend of espresso and nostalgia, greeted me like an old lover, drawing me into its embrace as I crossed the threshold.

"Bongiorno, signor Ferro," purred Maria, the proprietress, her voice dripping with honeyed warmth. "It has been too long since you last graced us with your presence, but I saw you on TV this morning."

"Did you now," I replied, my gaze lingering on the sinuous curve of her neck, the slender fingers that deftly made me a double espresso. "I find myself drawn back time and again, like a moth to the flame."

"Perhaps it is not the flame you seek," she teased, her eyes smoldering beneath a veil of dark lashes, "but the heat it provides."

"Ah, Maria," I sighed, allowing myself a brief dalliance with temptation before tearing my gaze away, focusing instead on the steaming cup of coffee that awaited me. "You know me too well."

"Too well, indeed," she murmured, retreating with a knowing smile as I settled into my favorite chair, its worn leather upholstery cradling me like a lover's arms. Here, in this hallowed alcove, I could be both observer and observed, a spectator to life's theater while remaining shrouded in its shadows.

"Sometimes I think I wear these shadows like a second skin," I mused, fingering the crisp lapel of my suit jacket, its material a cipher for the secrets I carried. "A cloak of anonymity to shield me from the world – or perhaps, from myself."

Sipping my espresso as I watched the café's patrons, their lives an intricate tapestry woven from threads of desire and deceit. They sought solace in the familiar, as I did, drawn by the allure of secrets whispered over steaming cups of coffee and glasses of wine gleaming like rubies in the dim light.

"Signor Ferro," a voice murmured, as mellifluous as silk sliding across bare skin. I turned and found myself ensnared by the gaze of an enigmatic café regular with whom I'd shared many an exchange over the years. "You seem to be lost in thought."

"Ah, Cesare," I replied, allowing his presence to draw me back from the precipice of contemplation. "I was just considering the intricacies of my latest case."

"Indeed?" he inquired, arching a single eyebrow in a manner that bespoke both interest and intrigue. "And what labyrinthine mysteries have you been untangling this time?"

"Human greed and power," I confessed, a bitter taste lingering on my tongue like the dregs of my espresso. "A tangled web of deception and betrayal, spun by those who would stop at nothing to possess both."

"Ah, but such is the nature of desire, no?" Cesare mused, his eyes gleaming like polished obsidian in the dim light. "It drives us to seek out that which we cannot have, to covet that which is forbidden. And in doing so, we often become entangled in our own webs of deceit."

"True enough," I conceded, the weight of his words settling upon my shoulders like a finely tailored suit. "But it's not only the guilty who suffer – the innocent are often caught in the crossfire, their lives forever altered by the machinations of others."

"Yet is it not our duty, as seekers of truth and justice, to ensure that those who would prey upon the innocent are brought to account?" Cesare countered his voice with a velvet caress that sent shivers down my spine. "To shine a light into the shadows and expose the darkness that lurks within?"

"Indeed it is," I murmured, feeling the familiar stirrings of resolve ignite within me like a slow-burning fire. "But at what cost? To ourselves and to those we hold dear?"

"Ah, my friend," Cesare whispered, leaning in closer so that our words were but breaths shared between us. "That is a question only you can answer."

And with that, he slipped away, leaving me to ponder the enigma that was my life - as complex and treacherous as the cases I sought to unravel. I wondered if, like the moth drawn to the flame, I, too, would eventually succumb to the searing heat of my desires.

The sun dipped low in the San Marino sky, casting languid shadows that stretched like seductive fingers across the ancient cobblestones. I stood at the edge of a literal and metaphorical precipice, my gaze tracing the curve of the horizon as it melted into the azure embrace of the Mediterranean Sea.

"Let go," I whispered to myself, the words slipping free like a stolen caress. "Let go."

A sudden gust of wind tousled my hair, setting my nerves ablaze with an electric shiver. It was as though life itself was urging me forward, compelling me to relinquish the past and step into the unknown. The sensation was heady, intoxicating – like the first sip of a fine Barolo after a day spent tangled in the sheets with a beautiful woman.

"I'll let go," I murmured, surrendering to the allure of possibility.

"Bravo, Luigi," a silky voice purred from behind me, sending tendrils of desire coiling through my veins. I turned, my heart skipping a beat as I beheld the familiar visage of Caterina, her raven locks cascading around her shoulders like a velvet waterfall.

"Ah, bella mia," I breathed, my pulse quickening beneath the weight of her smoldering gaze. "What brings you here?"

"Curiosity," she replied, her lips curving into a tantalizing smile. "And perhaps a touch of temptation."

"Isn't that always the way?" I mused, stepping closer until I could feel the heat of her body radiating against my own. "We seek solace in the shadows, only to find ourselves ensnared by our deepest desires."

"Perhaps," Caterina allowed, her eyes dark and fathomless as she reached up to trace my jaw line with an achingly tender touch. "But sometimes, the sweetest seduction lies not in the secrets we keep but in the truths we choose to reveal."

"Words of wisdom," I acknowledged, my voice thick with emotion as I reached for her hand, twining our fingers together like vines entwined along the sun-dappled walls of a hidden Tuscan villa. "But how do we know when it's time to let go – when it's time to step forth from the shadows and allow ourselves to be seen?"

"Ah, mio amore," Caterina sighed, leaning in until our breaths mingled like silk against satin. "Sometimes, the only way to truly let go is to trust – to trust that in the end, the light will always triumph over the darkness."

"Even in the heart of a man like me?" I asked, my eyes never leaving hers as the last vestiges of doubt flickered and died within the depths of my soul.

"Especially in the heart of a man like you," she whispered, pressing her lips to mine in a kiss that tasted of love and longing, surrender and salvation.

I put my arm around her shoulders and pulled her close.

The seductive call of my phone punctured the veil of tranquility that had enveloped me, its vibrations resonating against my chest like the throbbing heartbeat of a forbidden lover. I hesitated, reluctant to sever the fragile threads that tethered me to this moment of reprieve before surrendering to the relentless pull of obligation.

"Pronto," I murmured into the receiver, my voice heavy with the weight of duty.

"Signor Ferro! It's Madame Merola from the school,"

she said, her lilting accent akin to the gentle caress of silk on my skin. "I simply had to call you."

"Madame Merola," I replied, curiosity piqued. "To what do I owe this unexpected pleasure?"

"Our students have been captivated by your stories of intrigue and danger," she explained, her excitement palpable even through the cold embrace of technology. "And now, well... we seem to have caught something of a *Ferro fever*."

"Ah, sí?" I asked, a smile playing at the corners of my lips. "And how might I be of assistance in this epidemic?"

"Here is the surprising twist, Signor Ferro," she continued, her words weaving a tantalizing web of mystery. "One of our young students, inspired by your tales, has taken it upon himself to delve into an old case that has perplexed our faculty for years."

"Indeed?" I raised an eyebrow, curiosity piqued as echoes of my past adventures flickered in my mind. "And what is this enigma that has captured the imagination of your young protégé?"

"A professor who went missing many years ago," she revealed, her voice tinged with a mix of reverence and concern. "Professor Monti, a beloved figure here, vanished without a trace, leaving only questions and theories behind."

"Ah, the mystery of a disappearance," I mused, my thoughts traveling through the many twists and turns such cases often took. "A matter that often hides more than it reveals."

"Indeed, Signor Ferro," Madame Merola agreed, her

voice laced with a hint of urgency. "But this student believes he has found a lead that evaded the police and our own attempts at investigation. And we need your expertise to ascertain if there's any merit to his findings."

"Very well, Madame," I replied, feeling the familiar pull of a case unsolved, the allure of a puzzle waiting to be pieced together. "I shall make my way to your school and see what light can be shed on this long-standing mystery."

"Thank you, Signor Ferro," she breathed, relief washing over her like the gentle caress of an evening breeze. "We eagerly await your arrival."

As I ended the call, I found myself torn between the siren song of temptation and the unyielding call of work. For in that moment, I understood that the path before me was fraught with peril and desire – a journey that would lead me once more into the beguiling world of secrets and deception.

"Luigi," came the sultry whisper of Caterina's voice, her breath a sensual caress upon my ear. I turned to face her, my heart quickening as I took in the vision she presented – her brown eyes sparkling with mischief and desire.

"Ah, mia bella," I murmured, allowing myself a moment to drink in her intoxicating beauty. "That was just work?"

She moved closer, the faint scent of jasmine and bergamot enveloping me as she slipped her hand into mine. Her fingers felt like silk against my roughened skin, an exquisite contrast of textures that sent shivers down my spine.

"Am I not allowed to join you tonight?" she teased, her lips curling into a seductive smile. "Or is there some reason you wish to be alone?"

"Solitude has its charms, but sometimes even a hardened detective needs the warmth of human touch," I confessed, my gaze lingering on the curve of her neck, where the delicate lace of her blouse met her ivory skin. A wave of desire washed over me, threatening to sweep away the tenuous hold I had on my self-control.

"Then it is fortunate that I am here," she purred, drawing me closer still until the heat of her body seemed to seep into my very bones. "For I have always found your touch...most compelling."

As we walked toward her abode, I allowed myself a moment to savor the taste of her, the intoxicating blend of wine and desire that lingered on my tongue. It was a potent reminder of the life that awaited me beyond the shadows – a world filled with pleasure and temptation, where the seductive lure of secrecy blurred the lines between love and power.

THE END

LUIGI FERRO
WILL RETURN

A Story from

Yesteryear's Stories Reflected Today
Yabot AB
www.yabot.se

www.ingramcontent.com/pod-product-compliance
Lightning Source LLC
LaVergne TN
LVHW020341200726

843507LV00012B/2441